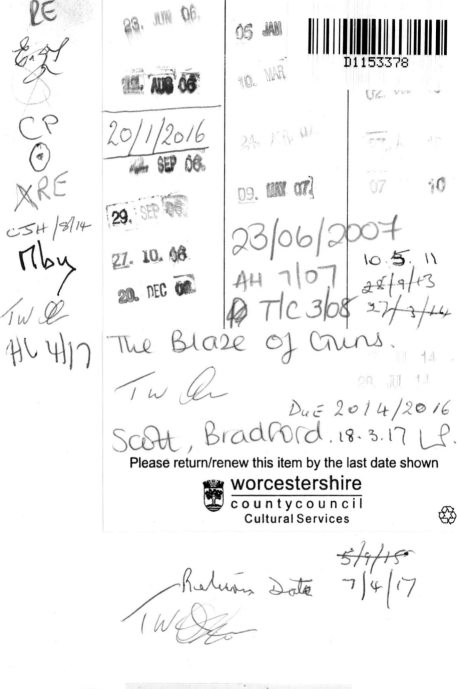

The Blaze of Guns.

Scott, Bradford.

Please return/renew this item by the last date shown

worcestershire county council
Cultural Services

Return Date

700025470152

THE BLAZE OF GUNS

THE BLAZE OF GUNS

Bradford Scott

Chivers Press • Thorndike Press
Bath, England   Waterville, Maine USA

This Large Print edition is published by Chivers Press, England, and by Thorndike Press, USA.

Published in 2003 in the U.K. by arrangement with the author c/o Golden West Literary Agency.

Published in 2003 in the U.S. by arrangement with Golden West Literary Agency.

U.K. Hardcover ISBN 0–7540–8945–2 (Chivers Large Print)
U.K. Softcover   ISBN 0–7540–8946–0 (Camden Large Print)
U.S. Softcover   ISBN 0–7862–4921–8 (Nightingale Series)

The text of this Large Print edition is unabridged.
Other aspects of the book may vary from the original edition.

Set in 16 pt. New Times Roman.

Printed in Great Britain on acid-free paper.

British Library Cataloguing in Publication Data available

Library of Congress Cataloging-in-Publication Data

Scott, Bradford, 1893–1975.
    The blaze of guns : a Walt Slade Texas Ranger western / Bradford Scott.
      p. cm.
    ISBN 0–7862–4921–8 (lg. print : sc : alk. paper)
    1. Texas Rangers—Fiction. 2. Texas—Fiction.
    3. Large type books. I. Title.
PS3537.C9265 B58 2003
813'.52—dc21   2002036014

CHAPTER ONE

Down in the big bend country of Texas, there is a trail—a gray and furtive trail that slinks and slithers, gliding into shadowy canyons, climbing chaparral clothed ridges, winding through bristles of thicket. It begins just west of the awful gorge known as Santa Helena Canyon, that bounds the Bend on the south, where the Rio Grande foams and thunders against the rocky walls, and continues through a vacant and silent land that belongs to the deer, the javelina, the panther and the bear, ever avoiding the sunlight, ever seeking the shadows. It is crooked and tortuous, but always its trend is northward. Its stones are black with dried blood, its thickets salted with the bleached bones of murdered men, for its history is a story of death and violence. It is shrouded in legend and tradition and knows many a grim secret. It is the old Smuggler Trail that leads from Mexico to the north.

It was an old trail when the Spaniard first set foot on Texas soil, old when the Aztecs thundered south by way of it, old, doubtless, before the Aztecs' time. In later days, the Comanches and Apaches padded over it on their raids into Mexico. Then came the cattle rustlers, the owlhoots and the smugglers who gave it its name, although the smugglers were

1

the last to ride it.

North, from below the Rio Grande, came the silver dobe dollars and other treasures to be turned into contraband goods that would be slipped back across the river, duty free, into Mexico, where there was a ready and profitable market for them. Customs officers, sheriffs and Rangers watched, and still watch, the Smuggler Trail. But the trail keeps its secrets well and its many branches and false leads, that dive into narrow canyons and gorges and thread their way through the little known hills, provide ways of escape for the lawbreakers.

South of a dark canyon that formerly had known death, a lone horseman rode northward on the Smuggler Trail. He was a very tall man, broad of shoulder, lean of waist and hips. Thick, crisp black hair showed under his pushed-back 'J.B.' A rather wide mouth, grin-quirked at the corners, relieved the sternness, almost fierceness, evinced by the prominent high-bridged nose above and the powerful jaw and chin beneath. His long, black-lashed eyes were clear gray in color—cold, reckless eyes that nevertheless looked out upon the world with laughter and found it good. Double cartridge belts encircled his waist and from the carefully worked and oiled cut-out holsters protruded the plain black butts of heavy guns. He wore the homely, efficient garb of the rangeland—faded blue shirt and overalls, vivid

2

neckerchief looped at his sinewy throat, scuffed, high-heeled half-boots of softly-tanned leather—and wore it with careless grace. He bestrode his magnificient black horse with the ease of a lifetime in the saddle.

Thus, singing gaily in his deep, rich voice rode Ranger Walt Slade, whom the Mexican *peons* of the Rio Grande river villages named El Halcon—The Hawk—'the friend of the lowly,' and of whom some folks, including more than a few puzzled law enforcement officers, said, 'If he ain't a owlhoot he's sure got plenty of people fooled, even if they can't never prove nothing on him.'

Shadow, the great black horse, suddenly pricked his ears forward inquiringly. Instantly Slade stopped singing and listened intently.

In the far distance sounded a thin crackling which the Ranger quickly identified as a stutter of gunfire.

'What in blazes?' he muttered. 'Sounds like a regular feuding!'

For some seconds, the sputter of shots continued, then ceased as abruptly as it began. A few moments later Slade, still listening, heard a single report followed by silence.

'And *that*,' he said to Shadow, 'sounded like a last survivor giving a final account of himself. Horse, I've a notion this will bear a little investigating, but take it easy, no telling what we may barge into. Funny things happen on this blasted snake track.'

He rode on, very much alert, listening and peering. And again Shadow pricked his ears. Slade tensed and his right hand dropped to the butt of the big gun swinging low on his right thigh. Quickly reversing the split reins, he made sure the heavy Winchester, snugged in the saddle boot beneath his left thigh, was free in its scabbard. He gazed expectantly ahead. His keen ears caught what Shadow had already heard, the loudening whisper of fast hoofs speeding from the north.

Around a bend in the trail bulged a foaming horse. On its back, reeling in the saddle, gripping the pommel for support, was a wild-eyed Mexican youth whose dark face was streaked with blood. He caught sight of Slade, slackened his horse's headlong speed and his hand flew to the gun at his belt.

'Hold it!' the Ranger warned in clear, ringing tones that stabbed like a rapier thrust through the fog that swathed the other's brain. 'Hold it! I'm not on the prod against you!' He made no move, but his eyes, abruptly cold as wind-swept winter ice, never left the Mexican's face.

The boy's hand dropped from his gun butt. He pulled his mount to a halt. *'Muerte Blanca!'* he gasped. 'May he burn in the fires of *infierno* forever!'

Slade's eyes narrowed slightly and he leaned forward in the saddle.

'What do you mean, the "White Death"?'

4

he demanded. 'What the devil are you talking about, *muchacho*?'

'Dead!' the boy moaned. 'All! All! My two brothers, my uncle and Don Miguel!'

'Take it easy,' Slade said, 'get a grip on yourself and tell me what happened.'

But the Mexican boy, with a choking sigh, toppled in his saddle and slid to the ground like a wounded bird from its perch.

Slade dismounted and knelt beside the half-conscious youth. With deft, gentle fingers he probed the jagged wound furrowing his scalp. Just creased, was his diagnosis, with no signs of fracture or concussion. Fainted from excitement and loss of blood. He stood up, strode to where Shadow stood and from his saddle pouches took a roll of bandage and small jar of antiseptic ointment. He returned to the boy, smeared the wound with the ointment and skillfully bandaged it. The other moaned under his ministrations and opened his eyes. They were quieter now, and his ragged nerves were smoothing out. Slade rolled a cigarette with the slim fingers of his left hand, lighted it and placed it between the boy's lips.

'Take a couple of good drags and you'll feel better,' he advised. 'Think you can sit up?'

The boy nodded, puffing hard on the brain tablet. Slade supported him with an arm until he was sure he was steady. He squatted on his heels and rolled another cigarette for himself.

'Now tell me straight what happened,' he said.

The boy began to talk, and he had the gift, not uncommon to the Mexican of much Spanish blood, of expressing himself eloquently. Aided by his own vivid imagination, the grim picture of what had happened spread before Slade's eyes.

CHAPTER TWO

Don Miguel Allende was a gay and imposing figure as he rode the Smuggler Trail at the head of his long train of heavily-laden mules. Black velvet pantaloons adorned with many silver conchas, tight fitting black velvet jacket embroidered with flowers in bright colored silk, scarlet silken sash, black steeple-sombrero encrusted with much silver, shiny black boots and huge silver spurs completed a costume well fitted to his lithe and sinewy form. Around his lean waist was a filled cartridge belt. The long-barrelled, ivory-handle revolver in its buttoned holster lent a grim note to his otherwise festive garb, as did the scabbarded machete hanging from his belt on the opposite side.

These contrasts were applicable to Don Miguel's character. He was equally ready for frolic or fight.

Behind the Mexican hidalgo's fine bay horse paced the mules, sturdy, sleek animals, well cared for, well trained. Don Miguel accommodated the gait of his horse to that of the mules, for the creatures carried no light burden. On their backs they bore great rawhide aparejos, the pack sacks the Texas cowboys called kyacks. They fitted snugly around the curving sides of the mules and were strapped securely beneath the belly.

The aparejos were stuffed with silver dobe dollars. Far to the north, Don Miguel would meet with certain merchants. The silver would go to swell the coffers of those same merchants, who grew rich on the trade in contraband.

But the pack saddles would not for long be empty. Soon they would bulge with goods of many kinds that would bring a handsome profit in Mexico. After they took the long trail back to Mexico there would be days of wine, women and three-card monte to follow.

Little wonder that Don Miguel smiled as he rode north along the old Smuggler Trail. It was a good life, the life of a smuggler, filled with adventure, romance and other good things. There was danger, of course, but the danger could wait. The stupid sheriffs and customs officers would swear, but they might as well set traps for the moonbeams or seek to corral the morning mists as to attempt pursuit and capture of wily Miguel Allende.

The same applied to *El Presidente's rurales*—the Mexican mounted police—below the Line. They would swear also, strange and colorful oaths, and Miguel Allende would laugh.

The Rangers? Well, that was something different, but the Rangers paid little attention to smuggling—that was the affair of the Federal law enforcement officers, unless Texas law was directly violated, and Don Miguel was careful not to violate Texas law.

And even should he, by some mischance, be captured here in Texas, his punishment would be light. For Miguel Allende was crafty. The goods he smuggled south were harmless merchandise that sought only to escape the nefarious tribute called duty. He was unlike the grim Muerte Blanca, who traveled only by night and bore south new rifles of the latest make and quantities of ammunition to arm, among others, his ruthless band he called, half in jest, half in earnest, his Army of Liberation. Muerte Blanca could expect little mercy from the gringos, and none at all from *El Presidente*, who hated and feared the pale-eyed killer.

Along the flanks of the mule train trailed the outriders, alert, hard-faced men, six-guns in holsters, rifles resting across saddle bows. Their vigilant eyes searched rock clumps and thickets for any hint of lurking danger. Constantly they scanned the brush-grown crests of the low walls that shut in the narrow canyon through which the Smuggler Trail slithered like a furtive snake.

The vigilance of the outriders increased as the canyon began to turn. They rounded a bulge of cliff and Don Miguel uttered a startled exclamation.

Instantly the riders surged forward, rifles ready for action. Then they too exclaimed, surprise and pity in their voices.

Sprawled on the rocky trail was a man, face-downward, his sandaled feet sticking out stiffly from the bottoms of his ragged trousers. His plain straw sombrero lay beside his tousled black head. His dingy serape was twisted awry on his shoulders. He lay motionless save for a heaving of his shoulders as he breathed in stertorous gasps.

Nearby stood a saddled and bridled horse, head hanging. One foot was raised from the ground, bending back from the knee joint. To all appearances the animal had a badly broken leg.

'One of our countrymen!' exclaimed Don Miguel. 'His horse fell and broke its leg and threw him. He is hurt. We must assist him.'

He moved forward. His followers trailed behind in a close group, their attention fixed on the body of the injured man. For the moment the trail ahead and the ominous brush-topped cliffs a score of feet above their heads were forgotten.

From the silent growth capping the cliffs

burst a roar of gunfire. Half of Don Miguel's men went down at that first murderous volley. Don Miguel reached for his buttoned holster. The vanity that caused him to fasten down the ornate flap was his undoing. Before he could free the weapon, the 'injured' man on the trail leaped to his feet, streaked two Colts from under his serape and sent a stream of lead hissing toward the demoralized smugglers.

Don Miguel fell without a sound to lie in a huddled heap. Again the rifles on the cliff top boomed. When the smoke lifted, riderless horses were galloping off in every direction. The burdened mules were squealing and bucking and trying to rid themselves of their loads. Don Miguel's men lay sprawled in grotesque attitudes. Only one moved feebly, groaning and retching, a slug through his stomach.

One other remained alive, the youngest of the band. He lay beneath a thick bush through which he had fallen. Blood streamed down his face from a gashed scalp, half blinding him. His senses whirled, his head was one vast throb, but he retained enough of consciousness to realize that his only hope for life lay in remaining concealed.

The man who had served as a decoy raised his voice in a shout.

'Okay!' he called to his companions on the cliff top. 'Come on down, pronto. They're all done for.'

Answering shouts sounded, then a crashing in the growth. A few minutes later a band of a dozen mounted men careened around the northern curve of the bend.

They were hard-eyed, evil-looking. Some were swarthy with the swarthiness of south of the Rio Grande. Others were undoubtedly from north of the river. In the lead was a tall and broad-shouldered man whose pale eyes glittered through the holes of a white silk mask that covered his face. His companions were unmasked.

'Get those mules bunched and moving,' he called in a clear, ringing voice. 'Take it easy with them, though; you can't push them, not with those loads, and we don't want them tumbling over from exhaustion. Take it easy, we're in no hurry. Nothing to worry about, and if anybody comes along, which isn't likely, we'll take care of him. Nice work, Brunch, you fooled them proper.'

The 'injured' man grinned crookedly, showing yellowish snags of teeth.

'Lucky for me I did,' he replied, his voice the harsh growl of a beast of prey. 'Was mighty glad to hear you fellers get into action before they got a close look at me and saw my horse's leg strapped up with that wire. It would have been curtains for me.'

He busied himself loosening the fine wires from about the horse's leg. The animal dropped its hoof to the ground with a snort of

11

relief.

The masked leader dismounted. He strode from body to body, peering into faces distorted by sudden and sharp death. He reached the wounded man whose features were twisted with agony. Drawing a gun, he placed it against the man's head and pulled the trigger.

'Can't take any chances with witnesses,' he remarked as he ejected the spent shell and replaced it with a fresh cartridge.

Under his concealing bush the sole survivor lay rigid with terror. He peered with dilated eyes through the mist of blood on his face and breathed prayers to his patron saint. ●

'What about the horses?' called one of the killers.

'Let them be,' replied the leader. 'No time to fool with them. All right, string out those mules and let's go.'

Around the bend streamed the grim band and the captive mules. Almost at once they turned aside into a split in the cliff, a split that would not be noticed from the trail by a casual passer for the stone overlapped the fissure much as does a folded sheet of paper. For a few minutes their horses' irons clattered on stones, then the group appeared on the cliff crest and sent the mules ambling across a broad level stretch that terminated at the foot of a long rise sloping upward to the distant skyline. Up the rise the laden mules progressed very slowly, for the going was rough and fairly steep. From where he lay the Mexican youth could see the creeping cavalcade drawing away from the canyon and the trail. Finally he crawled cautiously from under his bush and glanced about wildly, shuddering as his eyes rested on the sprawled bodies. He wiped the blood from his face with a shaking hand.

'*Madre de Dios!*' he moaned. 'Dead! All dead! May they rest in peace!'

The horses, well-trained animals, had not run far. Now they were nosing about and cropping the grass. The Mexican staggered to one, mumbling to himself. He managed to mount the animal, turned its head down canyon and sped south at breakneck speed. Behind him the laden mules and their captors slowly climbed the slope to the rimrock.

*   *   *

The words had fairly tumbled from the boy's lips and the telling of the grim story didn't take long. Slade listened patiently without interrupting till he paused breathless.

'And why are you sure the leader of the bunch was Muerte Blanca?' he asked.

'*Capitan,*' the boy replied. 'I saw the white mask with which he hides the features of *El Diablo.* I heard his cold voice. And none but that fiend of hell would shoot a man already wounded to death.'

'I see,' Slade nodded, the concentration furrow deep between his black brows, a sure sign El Halcon was doing some hard and fast thinking.

'You say the mules weren't making much time up the sag?'

'They were traveling most slowly, *Capitan*. The slope is steep.'

'Which way did they go?'

'Westward, *Capitan*.'

'And there must be a way up the cliffs from the canyon floor.'

'*Si*, a way difficult and rocky. I could not see but I could hear; the stones clattered.'

'A crack in the canyon wall, evidently,' Slade observed. 'And it all happened not much more than half an hour ago, wouldn't you say?'

'That is right,' the boy answered. 'Less than that time since they left the canyon.'

'And a hard pull up the slope,' Slade muttered, almost to himself. 'What's your name, *muchacho?*'

'Pedro.'

'I think I should be able to get a look at the hellions before they make it down the opposite sag,' Slade remarked. 'Okay, Pete, I reckon you're in good enough shape now to look after yourself. Take it easy!'

'You ride on their trail, *Capitan?*'

'That's right,' Slade replied as he mounted Shadow and gathered up the reins.

'I will come with you, *Capitan*,' the boy

14

exclaimed eagerly.

'Trail along after me, if you feel up to it,' Slade answered. His voice rang out, urgent, compelling, 'Trail, Shadow, trail!'

Instantly the great horse shot forward, steely legs shooting back like pistons, irons drumming the hard surface of the trail. Pedro scrambled onto his own excellent mount and started in pursuit, but Shadow drew away from him as if he were standing still.

'*Caramba*! what a *caballo*!' the boy exclaimed. 'And the *caballero* who bestrides him, ha! it can be no other! Today, Pedro, you have seen El Halcon!'

CHAPTER THREE

Into the gloom of the canyon Slade thundered, his eyes searching the trail ahead, roving over the wooded cliffs, probing thickets, missing nothing. His jaw tightened as he reached the scene of blood and death but he did not pause beside the sprawled bodies; there was nothing he could do for them. Without slackening speed he careened around the bend. Then his iron hand on the bridle pulled Shadow to a plunging halt.

'Turned off here, horse,' he muttered. 'Let's see—where in blazes did they go?'

The cleft in the cliff face was obscure, but

15

there were plenty of signs visible to the keen and experienced eyes of El Halcon to show which way the horses and the laden mules had gone. He quickly located the fissure and without hesitation guided the black horse into the narrow crevice. The track was steep and stony but covered only a short distance to reach the level mesa beyond. Still following the plain signs left by the quarry, he sent Shadow flashing across the level, reached the slope and went charging up it.

Shadow reached the crest with hardly slackened speed. Slade jerked him to a halt and in the same movement hurled himself from the saddle. Something yelled through the space his body had occupied the instant before. The hard metallic clang of a rifle sent echoes flying back and forth.

Not three hundred yards down the opposite sag were the mules and the owlhoot band.

'Back, feller!' Slade shouted to Shadow as he slid his Winchester from the boot. The black horse whirled and trotted back down the slope a few yards. Slade crouched behind a convenient boulder; his gray eyes glanced along the rifle sights.

Smoke spurted from the muzzle. The big gun bucked against his shoulder. One of the horsemen below whirled sideways from his hull and sprawled motionless on the ground. The long gun cracked a second time and a second man slumped forward with a yell of pain.

A clear command rang out. The riders unforked with speed and darted into the brush. A storm of lead whistled past Slade's sheltering boulder and smacked viciously against the stone. The Ranger crouched low, peering around the edge of the rock. Again and again he fired at stealthy movement below.

But the outlaws were well fanned out and they steadily drew closer. 'Getting sort of warm,' Slade muttered as he stuffed fresh cartridges into the magazine of his rifle.

His entire concentration focused on the advancing owlhoots, his ears dulled by the constant banging of his rifle, he did not hear the pad of light steps behind him. His first intimation that he was not alone behind the boulder was the boom of a shot at his very elbow. He whirled sideways with an exclamation.

'Oh, it's you, eh?' he said in relieved tones. 'Thought for a minute I was surrounded.'

Crouched beside him was the Mexican youth, rifle in hand. He nodded his bandaged and bloody head to Slade and pulled trigger again. An answering yell from below followed the report.

'Good man! Eyes like a hawk!' Slade said and fired at movement amid the growth. A curse slammed up from a bristle of bush that was suddenly violently agitated. Slade

17

chuckled as he worked the ejection lever. With two rifles going, the situation was vastly improved, from his viewpoint.

From their viewpoint the outlaws did not think so. Slade could hear their voices calling back and forth querulously, uncertainly. Then again the clear, ringing tones of the masked leader sounded. Slade could not quite catch what he said. The rifles continued to crack, but they were receding down the slope.

'Had a bellyful,' Slade grunted. 'We'll make it hot for them before they get those mules going again. If it wasn't so near dark we'd keep on trailing after them, but we can't risk it once the light gives out. They'd hole up and wait for us somewhere and blow us from under our hats. Get set, Pedro, and let 'em have it as soon as they come into the open.'

But the masked leader was a strategist as well as a man of action. The unseen rifles cracked. Puffs of dust spurted up at the very heels of the bunched mules. They snorted, brayed, headed down the faint track as fast as their burdens would allow. The horses followed more slowly, glancing back questioningly toward their hidden masters. They were nearly a thousand yards distant before the outlaws streamed from the brush to reclaim them. The form of the man Slade downed lay huddled in the trail, looking very small and lonely amid the vastness of the brush grown slopes.

18

With a Spanish oath the Mexican boy leaped to his feet and shook his fist at the departing outlaws.

'Look out!' Slade roared. 'Down, feller; *two* of those horses aren't forked!'

The warning came an instant too late. A rifle cracked. The boy gave a gasping cry and fell forward on his face.

Fire spurted from the muzzle of Slade's Winchester as he blazed away at the smoke puff, but he had little hope of scoring a hit. He swore under his breath as, far below, a man appeared from the brush.

'Plumb smart devils,' Slade growled. 'Left one hellion holed up to down us if we showed.'

The distant outlaw turned at that moment. A last ray from the hidden sun, reflecting downward from a cloud, fell on the white blotch of his face.

Slade swore again. 'The cold nerve of that sidewinder!' he sputtered.

The white blotch was not a face but a mask. The drygulcher who had lingered behind, waiting for a chance to shoot it out, was the tall leader of the band.

Confident there was nothing more to fear from the outlaws, Slade stood up and moved to where the Mexican boy lay. 'Poor devil!' he murmured pityingly. 'Reckon this does for his whole bunch.'

He stooped and turned the Mexican over on his face. Dark eyes stared dazedly into his.

19

'Well, I'll be darned!' Slade exploded. 'Your head will look like a patchwork quilt before you're finished. You must have a cannon ball for a skull. Just creased again.'

He wiped the blood from the boy's face, propped his scarred head on his knee. The Mexican swore feebly in two languages.

'They can't kill you,' Slade told him cheerfully. 'You'll live to even the score. Take it easy, now, while I patch you up a mite more.'

He whistled for Shadow, who came trotting up the slope. The antiseptic salve and the bandage roll were again pressed into service.

'Reckon that will hold you,' Slade said, giving the dressing a final pat, 'but try not to stop any more lead. I'm just about out of bandage. Well, it'll be dark in another ten minutes, so suppose we slide back down into the canyon, get a fire going and throw together something to eat. I've got coffee and some bacon and bread left in my pouches. I've a notion you could do with a couple of cups, steaming hot, about now.'

'*Capitan*, that would be wonderful,' Pedro replied with a wan smile. 'And if the *caballos* of my companions have not strayed too far, they also bear provisions.'

'Fine!' Slade applauded. 'We'll have a feast. First, though, I want to give that body down there on the trail a once-over.'

The body of the dead outlaw discovered nothing of significance—aside from a

20

considerable sum of money—except a crumpled slip of paper on which was jotted in very good handwriting a few words and figures. Slade studied it a moment, then slipped it into his own pocket.

'Just a notation of amounts advanced against wages by some cow outfit,' he told Pedro. 'The name of the outfit isn't mentioned, nor the fellow's name. I've seen this sort of thing before, usually made out by the owner for a man who wants a little money to tide him over to payday. I'll hang onto it—might come in handy. Could tie up this sidewinder with some spread, never can tell. Here, you take the dinero he was packing. I figure you've earned it. When we get to town we'll notify the sheriff of what happened and he can ride out and bring this carcass to town for folks to look at. Somebody might know him and who he was associated with.'

'*Gracias, Capitan,*' Pedro said, pocketing the gold and silver coins. He shook his fist at the darkening maze of canyons and gorges to the west and swore bitter vengeance against the killers of his relatives.

Leaving the body where it lay, they rode back to the canyon. When they reached its floor, Slade tactfully told his companion, 'You ride up the gulch a little ways and get a fire going, Pedro, I'll join you soon.'

The boy nodded his understanding. Slade rode down the canyon to where the dead smugglers lay. Without difficulty he caught the straying horses, removed their rigs and turned them loose to graze. He covered the bodies with the saddle blankets, secured some provisions from the pouches and rejoined his companion, who already had a fire going.

Slade quickly threw together an appetizing meal which they ate largely in silence. Then he rolled a cigarette and smoked thoughtfully for some time.

'Pedro,' he said at length, 'there's nothing more we can do tonight. As I said up on the ridge, there's no tracking those devils through the dark. We'll curl up here and go to sleep till daylight. Then I figure to make a try at finding where they headed to with their loot. If you care to come along, okay; but that's up to you. It may end in trouble, and the odds are against us.'

A hard glitter birthed in the Mexican youth's black eyes. '*Capitan*,' he said, 'I have the blood feud with those *ladrones*. That feud will never die until either I or they shake hands with *Amigo* Death.'

'Good man!' Slade applauded. 'Okay, we'll see it through together. Maybe we'll both have a chance to shake hands with the old gent with the scythe, but you never can tell.'

'I think,' Pedro said deliberately, 'that it will be a long, long time before you shake hands with him. Fortune favors the brave, *Capitan*.'

'And the devil looks after darn fools and

drunk men,' Slade smiled reply. 'Okay, let's go to sleep.'

Pedro did so at once, but Slade lay awake for a while, thinking grimly but nevertheless with some amusement of his interview with Captain Jim McNelty when the famous Commander of the far-flung Border Legion of the Texas Rangers dispatched his lieutenant and aceman on his latest chore.

*   *   *

'This "billy-doo,"' said Captain Jim, rustling the letter he held, 'sort of reminds me of something by a poet feller I read the other day. Don't remember perzactly how it went, but it was something like this—

"That nobody lives forever;
That dead men rise up never."'

Walt Slade chuckled. '"That even the weariest river winds somewhere safe to sea,"' he smilingly completed Captain Jim's misquotation.

'That's it,' nodded the Ranger Captain. 'Guess that last part is right, too. Reckon any river sooner or later reaches the home corral. But getting back to this letter, it says your old amigo, Muerte Blanca, is raising the devil, and shoving a chunk under a corner again, down in the Big Bend country.'

'What!'

'That's what the letter says,' Captain Jim repeated. 'It was writ by the sheriff down at Marta, Bert Wilson. A pretty good sheriff, too, I gather. I knew him quite a lot of years back. We worked together for the same spread. He admits he's licked and is yelling for help. Says it's Muerte Blanca, all right, white mask and everything.'

'Well, I'll be hanged!' Slade ejaculated.

'Quite likely,' agreed Captain Jim, 'only put it off a bit, if you don't mind. Meanwhile, I figure you'd better take a little ride down to Marta and look things over.'

So Walt Slade, in a very exasperating frame of mind, took a 'little ride,' following a circuitous route that would bring him to the cattle and mining town of Marta from the south.

And right off he had rammed slam-bang into something that precisely followed the pattern of the questionable activities of the Mexican bandit leader and revolutionary who over the course of the years had built up considerable of a reputation along the Rio Grande.

CHAPTER FOUR

The first light of morning found Slade and Pedro, awake. They threw together a breakfast and then mounted their horses and headed for the slope. Slade shook his head as they topped the crest and he gazed at the tangle of canyons and gorges beyond. Valleys and ravines crossed and criss-crossed, with the frowning bulk of mountains beyond, range on range piled higher and higher. Almost due west frowned the rugged Chiantis with the towering spire of Chianti Peak kissing the sky.

'Hole-in-the-wall country for fair,' Slade remarked. 'Well, here goes.'

The trail of the heavily-laden mules was easy to follow, for a time, for their sharp little hoofs cut deeply into the hard soil. The tracks led through a narrow canyon and then into a little valley grown with mesquite, creosote and sagebrush, with the eternal green of pinon and juniper crowning the slopes beyond. It diagonaled across the valley with a northerly slant to enter another and narrower canyon. Here the ground was stony but the sheer walls of the gorge made it impossible to go astray. Slade quickened their pace.

Still another gorge swallowed the canyon, and their troubles began. The ground was so hard and stony that even the feet of the mules left little or no imprint. The trackers slowed to a walk as they wound their way over the brush-choked floor.

Progress became irritatingly slow and tedious. Time and again they lost the trail and only regained it after a painstaking search. But a broken twig, a hoof-scarred stone or an overturned boulder was enough to put El Halcon on the right track again. On and on they toiled, under the burning sun. Noon came and went, the shadows turned from west to east and lengthened. And ever the trail wound steadily north with a slight veering to the east. Sunset was flaming above the crests of the Chiantis when they at last reached more open country and softer ground.

'*Capitan*, I believe we are gaining on them,' Pedro remarked hopefully.

But Slade was gazing ahead with a darkening face. 'Yes, I've a notion we are, but I'm also of a notion it isn't going to do us any good,' he said. 'I'm beginning to understand the reason for this packrat burrowing through the brush. We're coming out onto rangeland or I'm a lot mistaken.'

Another hour of steady riding over rolling grasslands with the western sky a glory of scarlet and gold and Slade pointed ahead.

Straight to a broad track, rutted and hoof-scarred, led the trail they had followed all day. Pedro uttered an exclamation and swore a Spanish oath.

26

'Yes, the Smuggler Trail again,' Slade said. 'I figured quite a while back we were paralleling it north and slanting toward it all the time. The hellions circled around through the broken country and came back to the Smuggler about thirty miles farther north of where they left it. That way they skirted the cattle spreads to the south of here and avoided the chance of meeting anybody. They knew the route and were able to make good time. Chances are they reached here a couple of hours after midnight. They wouldn't have to go nosing along like we have all day. They turned into the Smuggler where it is impossible to trail them and skalleyhooted to wherever they were headed for in the dead hours when nobody would be likely to be coming along.'

Pedro swore some more. Slade pulled to a halt on the edge of the Smuggler Trail. He scanned the beaten track and shook his head. The mule prints were lost among a multitude of other hoof marks.

'Ranches to the south and east, and some mines,' he remarked. 'Lots of travel up here. They've given us the slip, for the time being, anyhow. Well, let's go.'

They rode on north, Slade silent and preoccupied, Pedro staring ahead, vengeance written on his dark face.

Soon they began passing bunches of cattle. Slade noted that the brand was an RH. A mile farther on they sighted a ranchhouse to the east, small but new and tightly-constructed with outbuildings that appeared to be in good repair. Slade hesitated a moment, then decided against dropping in for a meal.

The trail flowed on. Just as full dark was descending, they passed a second ranchhouse much larger than the first and built in the Spanish style. It was set about a quarter of a mile off the trail and also to the east. Some cows they passed soon afterward bore a T Bar O burn.

'Prosperous section, it looks,' Slade commented. 'Now I wonder where those sidewinders headed for? Surely not to town.'

A couple of more miles and Slade slowed down and spoke to his silent companion.

'Pedro,' he said, 'something less than five miles to the north of here, according to what I've been able to learn of the section, is a town. We can make it by turning off to the right a little farther on. The Smuggler Trail continues to the northwest.'

'*Si, Capitan*, I know,' returned the Mexican. 'The town is Marta.'

'That's right,' Slade agreed. 'It's the county seat. I'll hunt up the sheriff and notify him of what happened in the canyon. He can ride down and look over the bodies and give them decent burial. That's all we can do for them. I want you to drop back before we reach the town and enter it by yourself. Those devils don't know they left any of your bunch alive,

28

and you are the only person who got a close look at them. Do you think you could recognize any of them if you got a look at them again?'

'A big man with red hair I think I would know,' Pedro replied. 'And one other, a small dark man with a knife scar across his cheek and nose, him also I would know. Muerte Blanca of course I did not see the face of. No one ever does. But the other two, *si*.'

'That's fine,' said Slade. 'It may help a lot. You slide into town and hang around. Don't tell anybody what happened down there. Got any money?'

'*Si, Capitan*, I have money.'

'Then you're all set. I took pretty good care of those scratches on your head and I don't figure you need to see a doctor about them. You can take off the bandages in a day or so. Just loaf around the saloons and places. Perhaps you can get a job as a swamper or dishwasher. That would give you a good chance to watch folks and listen to what's said. I'm playing a hunch that those sidewinders, some of them anyhow, will show in town sooner or later. It's a hangout for cowhands and prospectors and miners, and for gents who ride the Smuggler and other trails up from the south. You might learn something valuable. I'll get in touch with you at the right time. We've got to see this thing through. Those devils can't be allowed to get away with what they did.'

'I will see it through,' the youth promised grimly. 'And *El Dios* help those upon whose trail rides El Halcon, for to them man will be of small avail.'

'So you know me, eh?' Slade remarked.

The boy smiled faintly. 'Never before have I seen you, *Capitan*,' he replied. 'But who else rides the finest black horse in Texas? Who else sings as sing the angels in Heaven? And who else is so tall, so daring as El Halcon, the friend of the lowly?'

Slade chuckled. 'Thanks for all the compliments, *muchacho*,' he said. 'Hope I can manage to live up to them.

'One more word to you,' he added, the laughter abruptly gone from his eyes. 'Don't under any circumstances mention that you were with Don Miguel's smuggling train, or that you were anywhere around that canyon when the raiders struck. If you do and it gets to the wrong pair of ears, your life won't be worth a busted peso. Don't forget!'

It was well past dark when they drew near Marta, an almost treeless, jacal-fringed town which was a supply depot for the ranches to the north and south, and for a number of paying mines in the hills. To the northeast loomed the irregular, twisted mass of the Paracitas (little doors) Mountains. Mistily to the north were the Davis Mountains, with the Tierra Viejas almost due west. In the distance,

Marta was a cluster of tiny lights paled by the moonshine.

'Okay,' Slade told his companion, 'you pull up here at the forks and let me get to town before you make a move. First off I'll find a stable for my horse and some place to sleep. Then we'll see what's what.'

With a wave of his hand he rode on. Pedro waited in the shadow of a thicket, puffing on a cigarette.

Marta was still more than a mile to the north and better than two miles in an easterly direction by way of a trail that swept around through groves and thickets in a wide curve. As Slade neared the apex of the curve and turned almost due east, he heard, thin with distance, in the west, the wail of an approaching locomotive. He passed through a grove and sighted the twin steel ribbons of the railroad track gleaming in the pale moonlight. The trail paralleled the track which, a thousand yards or so ahead, vanished from sight behind a bristle of growth.

As Slade rode on, another whistle wail sounded, nearer. A faint mutter quivered the air, grew to a rumbling punctuated by the pattering exhaust of a speeding engine. Another moment and with a booming roar a long passenger train, headlight glaring, lighted coach windows glowing, swept past the lone rider and careened around the curve. Slade watched the bobbing red rear markers wink

31

out. Back to his ears came the rumble of the wheels and the staccato crackle of the exhaust.

Then abruptly the stuttering exhaust snapped off. There was a screech of brake shoes on tires, the drum of tightening couplers, a jangling of brake rigging. A grinding crash was followed by silence.

'Blazes!' Slade exclaimed. 'Sounded like she hit something!'

Even as his hand tightened on the bridle there came from beyond the growth a crackling of shots, then the boom of an explosion.

'Trail, Shadow, trail!' Slade shouted. 'All Hades is busting loose over there!'

The great black surged forward. A second explosion roared out. The banging of guns continued. Through the turmoil boiled the bellowing of escaping steam.

Shadow swerved around the curve at a dead run and a scene of chaos and hectic activity greeted Slade's gaze.

CHAPTER FIVE

The long train was at a standstill. The locomotive lay on its side, hissing and sputtering, steam billowing from a smashed cylinder, flames spurting from its burning cab. All about were scattered the boulders and heavy timbers of the obstruction into which the train had plowed. From the lighted coaches, that had miraculously remained on the tracks, came the yells, curses and screams of the bruised and terrified passengers. The express car careened drunkenly, its front trucks on the ground, its door smashed and splintered.

Even as Slade leaped to the ground with Shadow in full stride, something hurtled through the air, trailing a train of sparks behind it. There was a third booming explosion. The express car door flew to fragments. From the bushes flanking the right-of-way darted nearly a dozen men. Yelling and shooting, they rushed toward the express car.

Slade ran forward, a Colt bucking in each hand. The wreckers whirled with yells of alarm. A man pitched headlong, a second crumpled up like a sack of old clothes. A third reeled with a howl of pain and clawed at a blood-spurting shoulder. Bullets whizzed about Slade but, weaving and ducking, he still ran forward, returning the wreckers' fire with interest.

Passengers were boiling from the coaches. Somewhere along the line a gun cracked. A second joined in. From the express car gushed a stream of fire a yard long; the double boom of a shotgun joined the uproar. Yells of pain arose from those nicked by the flying pellets. Slade shot with both hands.

That was enough for the wreckers.

33

Bellowing curses, they dived back into the growth, Slade speeding them on the way with his last bullets. He stuffed fresh cartridges into the cylinders of his guns and ran forward a few more paces.

From the growth sounded a crashing and clattering of hoofs. Slade sent a stream of lead whistling toward the sound; the beat of hoofs steadily drew away.

Lowering his guns, Slade glanced about. The moonlight and the glare of the burning cab rendered the scene bright as day. A wild-eyed man disengaged himself from the group of milling passengers, flung up a gun and fired at Slade. The Ranger slewed sideways as the man pulled trigger; his own Colt spurted fire. The trigger-happy gent yelped and grabbed for his bullet-gashed hand. His six thudded to the ground a dozen feet distant. Slade's Colt flipped sideways and lined with a second man who held a gun.

'Hold it, you loco jughead!' Slade thundered at him. 'Everything's under control!'

The express messenger, flat on his stomach, was hanging out the car door, the shotgun still gripped in his hands. He added his warning to Slade's.

'That feller drove 'em off!' he shouted. 'Leave him alone, you blankety-blank fools!'

The pandemonium lessened somewhat. Slade holstered his guns and strode to the express car.

'You hurt?' he asked the messenger.

'Leg busted, I think,' the other gasped. 'Hurts like the devil. Nothing else, I reckon, Cowboy, you sure came along at just the right time. Oh, blast this leg! It burns like fire!'

'I'll take care of you in a minute,' Slade promised. 'Just lie still and take it easy. What were they after?'

'Better'n fifty thousand dollars in gold in the safe,' the messenger panted. 'They'd have had it if it wasn't for you, and I reckon I'd have gotten my come-uppance, too. That last charge of dynamite nigh to blew me through the wall.'

The conductor came hurrying up, lantern in hand, volleying profanity and questions. Slade cut him short.

'Get some passengers and try to beat out that fire in the engine cab,' he ordered the flustered trainman. 'Hurry up, the front end of the express car is already smoldering; your whole train will go up in smoke if you don't get the fire under control. Find out what happened to the fireman and the engineer. I'll look after this fellow who's hurt.'

The conductor hurried to obey. Just then a shout arose.

'Here comes another one!' the finger-skinned passenger whooped. 'Where's my gun?'

Menacing faces were turned toward the lone horseman riding swiftly toward the wreck.

Slade had no doubt as to who the rider was.

35

'Take it easy,' he told the jittery passengers; 'that fellow's coming up from the south. Everybody cool down, and keep your hands off your hardware. There's been too much promiscuous gunslinging around here already.'

Another moment and Pedro pulled his hard-breathing horse to a halt beside the wreck.

'What happen?' he called. 'Can I help?'

'Reckon you can,' Slade called back. 'Everybody else is too darn excited to be much good. Unfork and give me a hand with this man's broken leg. Find a couple of slats or something that will do for splints; there's plenty of stuff lying around that the dynamite blew loose.'

His face betraying no sign of recognition, Pedro obeyed, searching out some suitable strips from the mass of wreckage. Slade went to work on the injured messenger.

'Just the small bone broken,' he told him a moment later. 'I'll get the ends together and tie it up so it will do till you get to a doctor. There's no compound, so far as I can judge. Roll him a cigarette, *muchacho*, and light it for him. That will help.'

The messenger puffed grimly on the brain tablet Pedro manufactured while Slade worked over his fractured limb. A few minutes later he sank back with a sigh of relief.

'Feels a heap better already,' he said. 'Cowboy, you ought to have been a doctor.'

'The support provided by the splints keeps the broken ends from grinding together,' Slade explained. 'You'll be okay in a couple of weeks. Now I want to look things over.'

A quick glance told him that the trainmen and passengers had gotten the fire under control. He ascertained that the engineer and fireman had both jumped before the engine hit the obstruction and had escaped with minor cuts and bruises. The excited passenger he was forced to line sights with had lost some skin from his hand, half a thumbnail and the butt plate of his gun. There were no major casualties among the other passengers.

These matters settled to his satisfaction, Slade turned his attention to the two dead wreckers who lay sprawled by the track. One was a scrawny little individual. Across his rat face stretched the livid weal of an ill-healed knife slash. The other was big and bulky. His hat had fallen off to reveal a bristly head of flaming red hair.

Slade raised his eyes to meet Pedro's gaze. The Mexican youth nodded ever so slightly.

Slade grumbled disgustedly under his breath. Why the devil couldn't at least one of them have been another of the hellions! The only chance to recognize members of the drygulching band had gone a-glimmering. By a perverse spite of fate the dead men were the only two individuals Pedro had taken particular note of.

'The breaks went against us this time,' he told Pedro in low tones. 'The same bunch that drygulched your smuggling train, all right. But if the big leader was with them this time, he didn't wear a mask, or he stayed back in the brush, which doesn't seem likely.'

'*Muerte Blanca* always goes masked,' Pedro declared emphatically. 'His face none has ever seen.'

Slade did not comment but glanced over his shoulder toward the crowd of passengers who were busily discussing the wreck and sympathizing with the injured express messenger.

'Keep an eye on them and tell me if anybody heads this way,' he told Pedro. 'I want to give these bodies a quick once-over and see if they're packing anything that might prove interesting.'

A few moments later, however, he shook his black head. 'Not a thing that might tie them up with somebody,' he announced, adding, 'but at least here's some more money for you—stuff it in your pocket. Want you to be well-heeled as possible, so you won't have to hang on to a job if I happen to need you elsewhere.'

The conductor came hurrying up. 'We got the fire beat down,' he announced. 'Nothing else to do now but wait for the wreck train; but there should be somebody riding out from town any minute. They're sure to have heard the dynamite over there, and we were due in

Marta on time. When we didn't show up they'd know something went wrong.'

Slade nodded and walked over to the trail and gazed toward the twinkling lights of Marta. A moment later he spotted several blotches on the trail ahead. They quickly resolved to a band of speeding horsemen. A few minutes more and a group of riders dashed up and pulled rein beside the wreck. Foremost was a blocky old man with a drooping mustache and frosty eyes. He had a large nickel badge pinned to his sagging vest.

'What in blazes has been going on here?' he demanded as he unforked.

Everybody told him at once.

'Shut up!' bawled the sheriff. 'I can't make head or tail of all this gabbin'.' He turned to the conductor. 'What happened, Tom?' he asked.

'A bunch wrecked the train and made a try for the money in the express car,' the conductor told him. 'And if it hadn't been for this big cowboy here they'd have got away with it. He busted 'em wide open. I never saw such shootin'!'

The sheriff turned his cold gaze on Slade and eyed him from head to foot. 'A good chore,' he grunted. 'I'll talk to you later.'

He strode to where the dead owlhoots lay and peered into their faces. 'Never saw either of them before,' he said. 'Any of you fellers ever have?'

39

There was a general shaking of heads. The sheriff rumbled in his throat and tugged his mustache. 'Which way did they go?' he asked.

'Disappeared south through the brush,' said the conductor.

The sheriff turned to his companions. 'All right,' he said. 'We'll see what we can do. Fork your broncs.'

He hesitated a moment, his gaze lingering on Slade.

'I'm heading for town and a bed,' the Ranger told him quietly. 'I'll drop in at your office tomorrow. I have something else to tell you, but that can wait.'

The sheriff still hesitated, his eyes questioning; then he shrugged his shoulders. 'All right,' he said, 'I'll look for you. Stop at the railroad station when you get to town and tell them what happened. I reckon they've already sent for the wreck train, but I guess the express company will want to notify their detectives; not that it will do any good. All right, you fellers, let's ride.'

'His riding won't do any good, either,' snorted the conductor. 'Bert Wilson is a good old jigger and plenty salty, but the bunch operating in this section has got him pawin' sod and chasin' himself in circles. He's got about as much of a chance against Muerte Blanca and his hellions as a rabbit in a houndog's mouth. I don't see why they don't send some Rangers down here and clean

40

things up. They've asked for them and the section sure needs them. Nobody but the Rangers can buck Muerte Blanca, and he's a tough chore for even them. Been operatin' on both sides of the Border for years and nobody's ever been able to round him up. Guess you're about the first feller who ever bucked the sidewinders and sent 'em skalley-hootin'. But look out for yourself, cowboy, they'll be waiting for a chance to even up the score.'

With the admonishment, he stalked off to look over his train, growling to himself.

Slade glanced about but saw nothing of Pedro. The Mexican boy had doubtless made himself scarce upon the arrival of the peace officers. Slade was confident he'd slip into town and be on tap if occasion arose when he could be of help.

With a last word to the injured messenger and a promise to try and send a doctor along with the wreck train, he mounted Shadow and rode on to town.

'A nice section, all right,' he told the big black. 'If things keep on happening as they have in the past twenty-four hours, Captain Jim will be re-reading his poetry and wondering; and darn it! I can't blame him. "The witching hour, when grave yards yawn!" Beginning to look like it's always midnight down here! Well, first thing now is a place for you to put on the nosebag and hole up. Then I

41

can stand a bite myself and a little ear pounding. Sleeping on the ground is hard on the bones; I'll appreciate a decent bed.'

CHAPTER SIX

Marta proved to be a typical Big Bend cowtown, and a busy and prosperous one. Rows of false-fronts and some more substantial buildings lined its crooked main street, housing saloons, gambling houses, dance halls and general stores. The street lighting was inadequate but was amply supplemented by the glow from windows and the bars of radiance streaming over swinging doors. Marta evidently didn't go in much for sleeping, judging from the crowds on the street and the uproar coming from every place of entertainment. Long hitch racks flanked the board sidewalks and nearly every peg accommodated a horse.

Slade paused at the railroad station to deliver the sheriff's message and give a terse account of what happened.

'We've already ordered out the wreck train,' the telegraph operator told him. 'We knew something was wrong when the Limited didn't show up on schedule and we could see the light of a fire over to the west, after folks heard what they were sure was dynamite going off.

The wrecker should be here in an hour and I'll rout out the doctor and see that he gets aboard. You say the outlaws didn't get anything? Well, that's different from what they did last month with the westbound flyer this side of Marathon. They knocked off close to twenty thousand that time besides what they took from the passengers. Folks say Muerte Blanca pulled that one. Was there a feller wearing a white mask with the bunch tonight?'

'If there was, I didn't see him,' Slade replied.

The operator nodded. 'Well, reckon it wasn't Muerte Blanca's bunch this time, then. A place to put up your horse? Right down the next alley to your right; stable there. Tell Pete Henry I sent you. He's got one leg and the disposition of a gila monster on the prowl, but he knows horses and takes good care of them. He sleeps over the stalls and has a couple of spare rooms he rents out to fellers who look right to him. Wouldn't be surprised if he'd let you have one if you like to sleep close to your horse. And the Montezuma right down the street from the alley serves as good chuck as any, and the licker ain't bad, either. Always heard the games there are straight. And the girls—well, they all can dance. Much obliged for bringing in the word, cowboy.'

Leaving the garrulous operator, and chuckling under his breath, Slade headed for the livery stable. He had been observed riding in from the west and he found something of a crowd collected outside the station. Questions were volleyed at him which he answered briefly, refraining from making mention of his own part in the affair. Several men walked with him to the head of the alley.

'Must have been some salty jiggers on that train, to beat off Muerte Blanca and his bunch,' a big cowhand observed as they paused a moment.

'What makes you think it was Muerte Blanca?' Slade asked curiously.

The puncher shrugged. 'Who else?' he countered. 'They used the same system over toward Marathon last month. Ain't likely two such outfits would be maverickin' around in the section at the same time.'

Slade was forced to admit the logic of the deduction. He nodded and turned toward the lane. A moment later he knocked on the stable door.

Pete Henry, his red face framed in white bristles, looked cantankerous, all right, but the glance he bent on Shadow was distinctly approving.

'Uh-huh, reckon I can let you have a room,' he replied to Slade's request for lodgings. 'I don't usually rent to strangers, but a feller who rides a horse like that had ought to be all right. First door at the head of the stairs. It ain't locked. Here's a key to the front door. Try not to knock down the stairs when you come in

44

loaded. I sleeps light.'

Slade promised to come in quietly. He placed his saddle and other gear in the little room at the head of the stairs. It was meagerly furnished but was clean and boasted a wide window beside which grew one of the few trees Slade had noticed around sun-baked Marta. The tangle of leafy branches made a pleasing filagree against the starry sky. With a final glance around he left the stable in search of something to eat.

He had no difficulty locating the Montezuma, which proved to be a big combination saloon and eating house. There was a sizeable crowd lining the bar and occupying the gaming tables. Everybody appeared to be discussing the attempted train robbery. Curious glances were shot in Slade's direction as he walked to a table and sat down, but nobody approached him. Most of those present, he noted, were cowhands, or appeared to be, but Slade shrewdly deduced that some had not had recent contact with rope or branding iron. There was also a sprinkling of men who had the look of miners or prospectors.

The garrulous waiter who took Slade's order loafed around the table while he ate, and indulged in small talk relative to the section and its inhabitants. Slade let him run on in the hope of gleaning some information of value.

'Here comes Craig Telo and some of the T Bar O bunch,' the waiter suddenly announced as half a dozen men in range garb entered the room. 'The T Bar O is down to the south about seven miles or so. The ranchhouse sets off the trail a ways—big white casa built the way the Mexicans build 'em. Craig is a nice feller even if he is a bit wild. That's him in front.'

Slade was willing to admit that Craig Telo was undoubtedly a fine-looking man. He was about six feet tall with wide shoulders and a deep chest. His hair was raven black, but in contrast his eyes were light blue and his coloring was the golden bronze that only a very fair skin exposed to wind and weather is capable of attaining. His features were well marked and regular, his chin clean-cut, his mouth firm, thin-lipped. Slade thought he looked like he had some Spanish blood. His surmise was corroborated by the waiter a moment later.

'The Telos used to own a heck of a lot of this section, once upon a time,' remarked the talkative biscuit shooter. 'Old Manuel Telo, Craig's granddad, come up here from Mexico sixty or seventy years back. He was one of the real old Spanish Dons, I been told. He married a Texas girl and settled here, having an old grant to a lot of land hereabouts. His son married John Withrow's oldest gal, so Craig ain't got but a mite of Spanish blood, I reckon. Manuel and Craig's dad are both dead, and so's his mother. Craig was used to living sort of high when his dad was around and for a while after he passed on. But about two years back his troubles began. Manuel Telo held most of his land by way of an old Spanish grant the courts recognized, but his home spread, which ain't small, he bought from the state and of course his title to that was plumb sound.'

The waiter paused to bring an order to the kitchen, after which he sauntered back to Slade's table.

'Hope I ain't makin' you tired with my gabbin',' he remarked.

'Not at all,' Slade told him. 'I find it very interesting. What were you going to say about the Telos?'

'Uh-huh, about the rest of the Telo land, the big half of it,' resumed the waiter. 'About two years back a feller calling himself Rance Horrel showed up in the section, browsed around a bit and then disappeared.'

The waiter paused to bring Slade some more coffee.

'Did Horrel ever come back?' Slade asked by way of stimulating the conversation.

'Uh-huh, he came back, all right,' said the waiter. 'And then regular blue blazes cut loose. He had a lot of old papers with him. One of 'em said that old Manuel Telo had deeded most all of his south holdings to a Spanish soldier of fortune feller, for services rendered to the Mexican government—Manuel was a

Mexican citizen in those days, you know. Other papers said the soldier feller had sold it to a feller named Whitmer who lived in Boston. The papers sure looked okay. I rec'lect the deed to the Whitmer feller was dated 1867. Well, Craig Telo naturally raised the devil, but the court here decided the papers were okay. Didn't appear there was much doubt about Manuel Telo's signature on the deed to the soldier feller—sure looked plenty like his other writings that were brought out. Anyhow, the court decided it was his. Horrel had papers to show he bought the land from Whitmer. So it ended up that Horrel took over all the south holdings, leaving Craig only his home spread and the casa. That cut down Craig's income a heck of a lot, I'd say, but he still seems to have enough to gamble and lose like the devil and drink plenty. Funny about that land, wasn't it?'

'Yes, but there have been a number of similar incidents in the Southwest,' Slade said. 'I recall one where all the papers appeared to be in order except that a corner of the paper on which the grant was written was torn away, and that corner contained the signature of the Spanish governor who made the grant. The courts refused to allow the claim because the signature could not be produced. Then there was the famous Estancia Land Grants over in New Mexico, which was somewhat similar to the one you've been telling me about. There

48

were a number of killings before that one was finally thrashed out. And over in Arizona a fellow who called himself Baron of the Colorados showed up with a lot of old grants and deeds and cut quite a swath for several years. He was finally uncovered as a fraud, however, and went to jail. Seems that somebody discovered that the paper on which the deeds and grants were transcribed was manufactured by a Wisconsin paper mill that wasn't in existence at the time the papers were dated.'

The waiter nodded sagely. 'Uh-huh, and come to think of it, there was a newspaper feller, an editor of a paper over to Alpen, who took up for Craig and said Horrel was a phony and a fake from the word go; wrote some editorials about it. But I reckon the lawyer fellers hollered him down; anyhow he shut up after a while and the court ruled that Horrel's claim was okay. Reckon it was. I saw those old papers, over to the courthouse, and they sure looked all right. Funny-looking letters printed on 'em, the sort they used in the old days, I gather.'

'How come the papers are here instead of at the land office?' Slade asked idly.

'Oh, something about an appeal kept 'em here, I believe,' said the waiter. 'But I heard Craig has just about decided not to appeal the case. Figures it would be throwing good money after bad, I reckon.'

'Wouldn't be surprised,' Slade agreed rather absently, for his thoughts were more on the recent stirring events in which he had participated rather than the financial difficulties of the Telo family.

'Craig don't talk to Horrel, at least not nice, and I wouldn't be surprised if the row ends up like the one you mentioned, in a shooting,' the waiter remarked as he gathered up the empty dishes.

Slade observed that Craig Telo and his bunch were drinking together at the end of the bar and conversing in low tones. Once when he glanced up he caught Telo gazing in his direction, but as the bartender was talking to the T Bar O owner at the moment, he presumed that the drink juggler had mentioned that he, Slade, had brought the news of the train wreck and attempted robbery.

The T Bar O cowboys, he decided, had the look of capable hands and plenty salty. Both characteristics, however, were common enough among Big Bend punchers. Two very short men of bulky build and with a prodigious shoulder spread had the appearance of being brothers.

As Slade was finishing his coffee, the two short men left the group and sauntered out of the saloon. A moment later Telo also disengaged himself, walked to a table where a poker game was in progress and occupied a vacant chair.

'There he goes again,' observed the waiter at Slade's elbow. 'Craig's old man must have left him a hefty passel, all right, the way he throws it away on the pasteboards. The spread sure can't turn over enough dinero to keep him going the way he does. Seems to have gotten worse in the past few months. Plays till his poke's empty, then writes I.O.U.s that Charley Hansen, the owner, cashes for him. Always shows up to pay off when he said he would, though. Don't ever seem to lack for money.'

When Slade had sat down to eat, some time before, he had heard the wreck train boom past, headed for the scene of the disaster. Now the locomotive rolled up to the station again and halted with a screeching of brakes, bringing in passengers whose destination was Marta, Slade surmised. This was authenticated a few minutes later by new arrivals in the saloon who began discussing the happenings with other patrons. Slade abruptly found himself the recipient of interested glances. Apparently oblivious to the attention he attracted, he rolled another cigarette and smoked thoughtfully for some time. Finally he pinched out the butt and rose to his feet. He was feeling the need of a little shuteye after the stirring doings of the past twenty-four hours. Eyes followed his tall form as he sauntered out and turned up the street in the

51

direction of the stable.

A lantern hung on a pole near the mouth of the alley cast feeble gleams through the darkness. Under the tree beside the building the shadows were thick. Slade strode forward, humming under his breath.

It was his instinctive and mechanical attention to his surroundings that saved him. It was only the slight movement of a solider shadow in the gloom under the tree, but it was enough to send him leaping sideways in a hunching crouch against a building wall.

From the darkness under the tree gushed a stream of fire. A report crackled between the buildings and a bullet fanned Slade's face. He whipped out a gun and fired at the flash, instantly shifted position and fired again. An answering shot thudded a slug into the building wall. Slade fired twice, left and right, and glimpsed a dark form darting across the alley and into a narrow opening between two buildings. He bounded in pursuit, cocked guns jutting forward, dived between the building walls and out the opening on the far side. He found himself in what was apparently a backyard, across which a figure was speeding to dive into another opening. Slade snapped a shot at the fugitive and raced forward. Something struck him a terrific blow on the chest and sent him reeling back to fall heavily.

CHAPTER SEVEN

For several seconds Slade lay gasping, all the breath knocked from his lungs. Then he recovered his fallen guns and lurched to his feet, swearing feebly and caressing a burning weal across his breast.

'Hang a jigger, anyhow, who uses telegraph wire for a clothesline and strings it low!' he growled. 'Darn near cut me in two and let that hellion get in the clear. He either knew it was there or was a mighty short hombre to pass under it and not get slammed.'

With a disgusted oath he turned and retraced his steps to the alley. Just as he reached it, the stable door banged open and old Pete Henry appeared, his whiskers bristling, his peg leg pounding the boards. He held a lantern in one hand and a cocked Sharpes Buffalo gun in the other.

'Hold it!' Slade called. 'It's only me—Slade. Everything's under control.'

The proprietor let out a wrathful bellow. 'Didn't I tell you to come in quiet?' he stormed. 'And you have to go and shoot up the place! What you celebrating? Go way till you get sober.'

'I didn't start it,' Slade protested. 'Some horned toad was hiding alongside the door and threw lead at me when I showed. I threw some back but missed. He got away when I barged into a clothesline and knocked myself into the middle of next week.'

Old Pete let loose a string of appalling profanity and was instantly ready with an explanation.

'Trying to bust in and lift that black horse, eh? Well the varmint is mighty lucky *I* didn't get a chance to line sights with him. I don't miss and this old base burner would blow a team of oxen through a brick wall.'

He waved the Sharper threateningly as he spoke. Slade saw the miniature cannon was still at full cock and ducked out of range.

'Put down the hammer,' he told Henry. 'You'll blow the building away if that thing goes off.'

Henry lowered the hammer and tucked the fifty-calibre under his arm.

'Come in and shut the door,' he growled, 'before somebody comes snoopin' around to see what all the shooting was about and starts asking darnfool questions. Come on, I want to get some sleep tonight.'

He locked the door after Slade and stumped angrily up the stairs. Slade went to his own room, lit the bracket lamp and examined his sore chest. Concluding that the taut wire had done no noteworthy damage, he rolled a cigarette, sat down on the bed and gave himself over to some serious thought.

Well, they had spotted him in a hurry. No

wonder, though, with folks barging in from the wreck and gabbing their heads off. But just who was the lead slinging gent and where did he stand in the set-up? Did the bunch have somebody stationed in town? Or did they slip back into town after the abortive try for the express car money. Didn't seem reasonable, but it was not impossible. Would have been a nervy but smart trick to slide in while the sheriff and his posse were hightailing to the wreck. In the general excitement, men riding in by twos and threes wouldn't have attracted any attention. That *could* be the explanation.

Of course the devils had gotten a look at him down on the ridge above the canyon, enough to notice his height and the color of his horse. That, too, could be the answer. And there was no doubt in his mind but that the same bunch pulled both jobs. It was highly unlikely that two different outfits could boast such an ill-mated pair with distinctive features as the dead wreckers.

Well, it was a salty bunch with plenty of savvy, and it was up to him to find answers to the questions if he wanted to stay alive. He wondered how Pedro had made out and hoped to run into him in the morning. The Mexican boy was alert and intelligent, and obsessed as he was with a desire to avenge his slain relatives, he might be of considerable help.

Outside the window the tree limbs tossed and groaned as the wind made an eerie, heart-chilling music in the branches. The leaves rustled with a stealthy, menacing sound through which seeped the mutter and grumble of Marta's night life.

'I'm getting jumpy,' Slade told himself as he extinguished his cigarette and tossed the butt out the window. He cleaned his guns, put out the light and went to bed.

*　　　*　　　*

Sometime during the night, Walt Slade had a vivid and disquieting dream. It seemed to him the wind had risen to hurricane proportions. He could hear it tossing the branches and beating them against the wall of the building. Limbs broke with a sharp snapping sound. One hurtled through the window and thudded on the floor. The leaves rustled with a hissing sound as of a giant and angry serpent. Lightning flickered, but there was no thunder, only the eerie and continuing hissing. Nature seemed to be gathering her forces for some tremendous outburst.

Suddenly Slade's eyes snapped open. He sat up in bed, wide awake, staring at the window. Outside there was no sign of wind; the branches were still, the leaves, with the light of the street lantern glinting on them, hung motionless.

But that stealthy and menacing hissing continued, and there was a flicker of light in the room, as if from distant lightning flashes.

The sound appeared to come from the direction of the window, although Slade could see nothing there; his glance dropped to the floor beneath. Another instant and he bounded out of bed and rushed to the window.

On the floor beneath the ledge was a spurting of golden sparks that crept steadily over the floor, giving out the hissing sound as of an aroused snake.

Slade dived for the fiery serpent, groping about frantically, his fingers closed on a fat, greasy cylinder. With a gasp he plucked the capped and fused dynamite stick from the floor, leaned out the window and hurled the sputtering death down the alley with all the strength of his arm.

There was a blinding flash, a terrific roar. Slade was slammed backward to the floor. Glass from the shattered window panes rained over him. The building rocked and shivered till he was sure it would collapse in ruin. Outside was the thud and clatter of falling objects. Yellow, acrid smoke drifted in through the window.

Half stunned, his head whirling, Slade scrambled to his feet, clutching the window ledge for support. From the stalls below came the stamp and scream of frightened horses. In his room next to Slade's Pete Henry was bellowing profanity. A moment later Slade heard his peg leg thumping the floor.

Outside sounded shouts, drawing nearer, and the pad of running feet entering the alley. Slade realized that old Pete was pounding on the door and demanding admittance. He hastened to shoot the bolt and fling it open.

'What in blazes happened?' bawled the stable keeper. 'Did you hear it? What was it, an earthquake?'

'Sounded like a dynamite explosion in the alley,' Slade replied, wiping the cold sweat that beaded his face. He strode back to the window, peered out, and abruptly realized that his dream of branches breaking in the wind was no dream, after all. One stout limb that brushed the side of the building had been snapped off short. He instantly understood just what had taken place.

The snake-blooded devil had shinned up the tree, swarmed out on the limb till he could reach the window. He lit the fuse and just as he was easing the lethal charge into the window, the branch broke under his weight. It was a miracle that the capped dynamite didn't explode when it hit the floor. Slade fervently hoped the hellion busted his neck when he fell. This was getting a bit too interesting for comfort.

Outside, a crowd was milling in the alley. Lanterns began to flicker.

'Let's go down and see if we can find out what the blankety-blank happened,' suggested Henry.

Slade threw on some clothes and they descended the stairs together, pausing to soothe the frightened horses. Outside the crowd was being constantly augmented by new arrivals who grouped around a sizeable and still smoking crater. The whole wall of a flimsy warehouse building had been blown in by the blast.

'Why in blazes would anybody want to use dynamite to bust into that shack?' a voice was loudly demanding. 'It belongs to the Givens General Store and there ain't nothing in there but canned goods and sacks of beans.'

There was no satisfactory answer to the question, although many wild suggestions were offered, none of them acceptable.

'Reckon a loco drunk figured it's Fourth of July,' somebody hazarded. 'Wonder where it blew him to?'

'Maybe the train wreckers got mad and figured to blow up the town to even up for the dinero they didn't get from the express car,' somebody else remarked.

This explanation was scoffed at as highly improbable.

Slade kept in the background, not wishing to attract attention to himself at the moment.

'Guess we might as well go back to bed,' he said at length to Henry. 'Nothing to learn down here.'

'Yes, reckon we might as well,' agreed old Pete. 'Confound it! Won't I ever get any sleep tonight? And I'll be busy all day mending busted windows. Wouldn't be surprised if that feller was right—some drunk figuring to act funny. That's my guess, too.'

Slade did not differ with him and they returned to their rooms after a few more comforting words to the horses and making sure they had suffered no hurt.

Old Pete creaked down on his bed a few minutes later, but Slade sat for some time beside the open window, which now was very much open indeed, not a whole pane remaining in the sashes and the sashes themselves were pretty well splintered. He realized he was up against as ruthless and ingenious an outfit as he had ever encountered, and one of determination and persistence.

And the worst part of it was he hadn't the slightest notion who they were. He had figured that the White Death with his bizarre mask was just a cover-up for a regulation brush-popping robbing and wide-looping bunch, but now he was beginning to wonder. Just why were they so darned anxious to rub him out? Revenge for the trouble he made them? It didn't seem reasonable. Might explain the attempt to drygulch him, but painstakingly and dangerously keeping it up to the extent of trying to blow him through the ceiling hinted at a more serious motive. It appeared somebody was extremely anxious to get rid of

60

him, but why? The logical conclusion was that somebody, or several somebodies, were scared he might catch onto something. Again the logical assumption was that somebody was playing a part that so far had not been ascribed to him. Slade believed it was so. Of course they might have recognized him as a Texas Ranger. But even that hardly explained things. A regulation owlhoot bunch would just try to keep in the clear rather than take a desperate chance that might open up a trail. It appeared he had given somebody a terrific jolt. It was not at all unlikely but that he had been recognized as El Halcon with a reputation for horning in on good things other people had gotten going, but that did not altogether explain the furtive undercover methods employed against him. If they considered El Halcon a meddling outlaw, a direct attack on him would be the likely procedure. Any owlhoot was fair game and if a man with such a reputation got downed, nobody would pay it much mind.

Slade hoped he had been recognized as El Halcon, whom many people considered an outlaw or mighty close to being one. More than once in the course of his Ranger activities he had found the dubious reputation he had built up through sometimes operating undercover, and not revealing his Ranger connections, to his advantage. Among other things, it opened up avenues of information denied a known peace officer. That it also meant deadly danger to himself he dismissed with a shrug of his broad shoulders. All in the game, and if your number isn't up, nobody can put it up.

Comforted by this somewhat dubious philosophy, he went to sleep.

CHAPTER EIGHT

It was the sun, peeping over the roofs and pouring golden rays into the room that awakened Slade in the late morning. For a while he lay listening to old Pete grumbling and hammering around his broken windows. Finally he arose, dressed and descended the stairs. He enjoyed a shave, and a sluice in the cold water of the big trough in the back of the stable, after which he repaired to the Montezuma and a leisurely breakfast.

Next he located the sheriff's office. Sheriff Bert Wilson was seated at his desk and looking very disgruntled. He nodded to Slade and indicated a chair.

'Have any luck?' the Ranger asked.

'None at all,' grunted the sheriff. 'We trailed 'em south a ways, but they turned into the Smuggler below the forks and there was no tracking them after that, especially by moonlight. We did ride south quite a piece on the chance that they headed that way, which I reckon they did, but didn't see hide nor hair of them. Right after we got back into town somebody blew a hole in Givens' warehouse for no reason at all that anybody can figure. The whole section 'pears to be going loco. You say you have something to tell me?'

Slade narrated his experience in the canyon the day before. The sheriff swore in weary disgust.

'I'll send a deputy and some jiggers with picks and shovels down there,' he promised. 'Smugglers ain't overly desirable citizens, but they hadn't ought to be shot down in cold blood. Smuggling is against the law, but folks don't pay it much mind down here. More than one reputable businessman got his start slipping stuff across the Rio Grande. I've a notion that was Miguel Allende's outfit. Miguel wasn't a bad sort and he always managed to keep from getting caught. Never went in for anything but running goods. Different from Muerte Blanca and his sidewinders.'

'Just who do you figure Muerte 'Blanca to be?' Slade asked.

Sheriff Wilson shrugged his shoulders. 'Just *who* he is nobody ever has seemed to know,' he replied. 'But what he is there ain't no doubt about. He's a blasted Mexican bandit who operated down below the Line for a long time and now and then slid over into Texas to cut loose with some devilry. He's got a big following the other side of the Rio Grande. It's only in the past few months that he got going strong this side of the Border. For quite a while, maybe a year, there wasn't nothing heard of him, then all of a sudden he busted loose and has been swallerforkin' ever since. He's bad and he's smart, nobody realized just how smart until of late.'

'Very likely,' Slade agreed dryly. He fixed the full force of his level gray eyes on the sheriff's face. 'Muerte Blanca, the Mexican bandit and revolutionary, died in Mexico more than a year ago.'

'Uh-huh, I heard that yarn, too,' the sheriff answered incredulously.

'It's true,' Slade said.

'How do you know it's true?' demanded the sheriff.

'Because I killed him.'

Sheriff Wilson jumped in his chair. 'What?' he exclaimed.

'That's right,' Slade answered.

The sheriff's eyes turned a bit glassy. 'How—how come you killed him?' he sputtered.

'He reached,' Slade replied laconically.

The sheriff gulped in his throat and looked dazed. Then he remarked, with apparent irrelevance, 'I used to hear folks say the fastest gunhand in the whole Southwest belonged to Muerte Blanca.'

64

'Maybe.'

Suddenly the sheriff leaned forward and his gaze was hard on Slade's face.

'And,' he said softly, 'there are folks who 'low that a jigger the Mexicans call El Halcon has the fastest gun hand that ever growed in Texas.'

'Maybe.'

Sheriff Wilson slumped back in his chair and swore an exasperated oath.

'But if you didn't dream up what you just told me, who in the blinkin' blue blazes is the hellion setting up to be Muerte Blanca?'

'That,' replied Slade, 'is a question to which I wish I had the answer, and haven't.'

The sheriff swore some more. To make him feel better, Slade regaled him with an account of the two attempts on his life the night before, which provoked more official profanity.

'So that's what the dynamiting was about,' Wilson growled. 'And they tried to gun you, too? Son, they're hard on your trail and it's a bad bunch.'

Slade shrugged. 'Sort of,' he conceded. 'I've a notion the jigger who took the shot at me was getting ready to climb the tree right then. When I spotted him he took off, but he came back. Persistent devil with plenty of nerve. And you say you trailed the wreckers to the Smuggler Trail?'

'That's right,' agreed the sheriff.

'And couldn't tell for sure whether they

65

turned south or north.'

'Right again, but I figured south. Hole-in-the-wall country down there.'

'Which may have been what they figured you would do,' Slade remarked thoughtfully.

'What do you mean by that?' asked the sheriff.

'Nothing much,' Slade replied. 'Only I'm pretty sure that a couple of the bunch, maybe more, were pretty hard hit. Badly wounded men don't make for fast riding and you were on their trail mighty soon after they pulled out. They might have headed for a nearby hole-up where the wounded men could receive attention.

'You mean here in town?'

'Could be,' Slade admitted.

'I hardly think so,' said the sheriff, 'but you could be right.'

At that moment the door opened and a man entered, a tall, well-formed man wearing a pleasant smile. He had comely features and keen deep-set eyes of a gray even lighter than Slade's.

'Howdy, Horrel,' grunted the sheriff. 'What's on your mind?'

'More trouble,' Horrel replied in a clear, nicely modulated voice.

'Nobody ever brings me anything but trouble,' growled the sheriff. 'Now what?'

'Twenty head of improved stock run off my east pasture three nights back,' Horrel announced.

'Why didn't you bring me word before?' asked the sheriff. Horrel shrugged his broad shoulders.

'What was the use?' he countered, rather pointedly, Slade thought. 'The rustlers had many hours start. It was a cold trail. I brought a list with me that describes the cows, on the faint chance that they might have been disposed of somewhere in the section, although I fear that isn't likely.'

'Darned unlikely, I'd say,' said the sheriff. He took the list and began studying it. Horrel sat down and shot an inquiring glance at El Halcon.

'Slade, I want you to know Rance Horrel who owns the RH spread to the south of Craig Telo's holdings. Rance, this is Walt Slade, who rode into town last night, the feller who busted up the train robbery.'

'Glad to know you, Slade,' Horrel said, shaking hands with a firm grip. 'You did a good chore, a mighty good chore. I heard about it and hoped to meet the man who gave those hellions a larruping.'

Slade nodded, his eyes thoughtful. He was not thinking of Horrel's conventional compliment, but what the sheriff said a moment before. For Slade did not recollect mentioning his first name to Sheriff Wilson.

After a few more remarks, Horrel took his departure, nodding pleasantly to Slade. The sheriff shot an exasperated glance after his broad back.

'A nice jigger,' he said, 'but the way he has everything at his fingertips is the limit. Every time he loses some cows, and he's lost quite a few, he brings in a detailed description of them. He sure runs his place right up to the hilt, which is more than can be said of the man he got the land away from. Craig Telo is too darn easygoing where business matters are concerned for his own good; but Horrel can tell you how many hairs there are on any cow he owns. And he drives a sharp bargain. Absolutely a squareshooter, though. When he says he'll do something you can depend that it'll be done just exactly as he promises. Not the skinflint type you'd expect from that kind of a jigger, either. Good spender, and I've heard he never turns down anybody who asks a favor. Drinks some, but not too much. Gambles some, but not too much. If he's got any other bad habits, nobody has been able to notice them.'

'Altogether, a desirable citizen, it would seem,' Slade remarked.

'Yes, he's all of that,' the sheriff agreed. 'But I've a notion he can be plenty salty if necessary, and Craig Telo will do well to lay off him.'

'Been trouble between him and Telo over the land deal?'

'Craig made some threats,' the sheriff

replied. 'I told him to tighten the latigo on his jaw and he got pretty huffy with me. Craig thinks the whole section is down on him, which isn't so. It's just that the matter was settled in the court in an orderly manner. Judge Arbaugh said that it appeared to be an open-and-shut case in Horrel's favor, that Craig could not bring forward any evidence to refute the validity of the deed, which he was convinced was authentic. The way is open for Telo to appeal, of course, but even his own lawyer appears reluctant to carry the case any farther. I don't know whether Craig will listen to reason. He's wild and hotheaded and always has been. Worse since the row over the land. And he spends money like water.'

'He must have been left quite a good deal by his father, then?'

Sheriff Wilson appeared reluctant to answer the question, but finally did. 'Craig is a secretive sort of a cuss and never discusses his business affairs with anybody, but so far as I've been able to learn he spends more than he was left.'

'More than his spread brings in?'

Again the sheriff hesitated. 'It looks sort of that way to me.'

'And what's the answer to that?' Slade persisted.

'I don't know,' the sheriff admitted.

'I see,' Slade said thoughtfully.

The sheriff rose to his feet. 'Well, I'll corral

a deputy or two and some grave diggers and amble down to that canyon,' he announced. 'We'll have an all night ride back, but I'm used to that of late.'

'And be sure and pack along that body you'll find over the other side of the ridge,' Slade said. 'Somebody in town might recognize the hellion and tie him up with something or somebody.'

'That's a notion, all right,' the sheriff conceded.

'And by the way,' Slade remarked, 'just who told you I was El Halcon?'

'It came to me in a sort of roundabout fashion,' the sheriff explained. 'A bartender over at the Root Hog heard one cowhand tell another that somebody had told him a feller said the notorious outlaw El Halcon was squatting in our midst, and that the feller who busted up the train robbery was El Halcon.'

'You don't appear much worked up about it,' Slade observed smilingly.

'I'm not,' the sheriff answered, 'but I'm mighty glad to see you here. I'd begun to believe old Jim McNelty had plumb forgotten me.'

CHAPTER NINE

It was Slade's turn to stare. 'And how the devil did you guess that?' he demanded.

'Oh, just put two and two together and made five instead of four,' said Wilson. 'I know how Jim works and I'd been told that El Halcon was seen around the Ranger Post every now and then, which was sort of funny for an owlhoot.'

'Sheriff,' Slade chuckled admiringly, 'you're smart.'

'But not smart enough,' sighed the sheriff. 'Otherwise I wouldn't have had to ask for help.'

'Just what did you do for a living before you got to be sheriff?' Slade asked.

'I was a cowhand,' replied Wilson. 'Got appointed a deputy, then later ran for the office when old Sheriff Conroy decided to call it quits. Won the election, and I'm beginning to wish I hadn't.'

'So you see,' Slade said gently, 'you never had a chance to get the extensive training a Ranger gets. Plenty of courage and a fast gunhand isn't enough to cope with such matters as have developed here. It requires a knowledge of outlaw ways and manner of thinking and the ability, gleaned from experience, to anticipate what the outlaw plans to do, and to forestall him in time, for a peace officer to be successful in such a situation.'

'I guess you're right,' Sheriff Wilson agreed soberly. 'Anyhow I know I haven't been having any luck. If I could just come to grips with the hellions—'

'Then it would be too bad for the hellions,' Slade finished the observation. 'Well, if I can just get a break or two, maybe you'll get the chance, and if you do, I figure I can depend on you till the last brand is run. Captain Jim has a good opinion of you, I know that. He talked about you quite a bit. Said among other things that I was liable to have trouble convincing you I am a Ranger, if I thought the time had come when it was expedient for you to know. He said you never would believe anything. Like the time when you and he were riding line for the Scab Eight and he told you there was a skunk in the meal bin and you wouldn't believe him and had to find out for yourself.'

'Why that infernal old liar!' exploded the sheriff. 'He told me there was a rabbit in there he was saving to cook for supper. Told me to haul it out. I reached in and grabbed that blasted pole-cat by the tail. If my eyes hadn't been so full of fog, Jim McNelty would never have lasted long enough to be a Ranger Captain. I missed him twice as he went out the door!'

Slade shook with laughter. 'He didn't tell it just that way,' he conceded. 'I'll have to ask him about it. I gather Captain Jim was quite a prankster in his day.'

'He was all of that,' said the sheriff. 'I could tell you by the hour the things that hellion used to do when he was a young feller. And I've a notion he ain't altogether got over it yet. I'll never forget the time old Nate McCoy was sittin' in a chair so dead drunk he wouldn't have known it if the roof caved in on him. There wasn't anybody much around at the time, so Jim got a hammer and nailed Nate's boots to the floor. After a while Nate sort of come to and tried to stand up; couldn't move either foot. He let out a screech that shook the rafters and yelled he had creepin' paralysis and that they were working up his legs and when they reached his heart he'd be a goner.

'His son, Bob, a big husky young gent, came rushing across the room and tried to set the old man on his feet. Lifted Nate plumb out of his boots. It took seven snorts of redeye to get Nate back to normal.'

Slade laughed again. 'It sure *is* a wonder he lived long enough to be a Ranger Captain,' he conceded.

'You can say that again,' grunted the sheriff. 'Well, guess I'd better be riding if I want to get to that canyon before dark. See you when I get back. By the way, how did an educated gent like you happen to get in with the Rangers?'

'There are quite a few educated men with the Rangers,' Slade replied. 'In my case it was

73

a series of unfortunate incidents that caused me to sign up with Captain Jim. You'll recall the droughts and blizzards that plagued the Panhandle country a few years back. It hit plenty of cattlemen hard, including my father. The year I graduated from a college of engineering, he lost his spread. Just about broke his heart to lose the old place and I'm sure it was responsible for his death shortly afterward.'

'Wouldn't be surprised,' nodded the sheriff. 'Hard on an old jigger to see what he's worked all his life for peter out.'

'Well, I was left sort of at loose ends,' Slade resumed. 'I'd planned to take a postgraduate course in special subjects to round out my education before starting to work at my profession. That, of course, became impossible at the time. I'd done some work with Captain Jim during summer vacations and when he suggested I sign up with the Rangers for a while and pursue my studies in spare time, I thought it was a good notion.'

'Did you pursue 'em?' Wilson asked.

Slade nodded. 'Yes, and quite a while ago I'd gotten more than I could have hoped for from the post-grad. I still keep after my books.'

Sheriff Wilson shot him a shrewd glance. 'All set to be an engineer then, eh? Why aren't you?'

'Well,' Slade smiled, 'I'll have to admit that Ranger work has sort of gotten a hold on me.

I'm young and there's still plenty of time to be an engineer, which I intend to be. Now, however—'

'In other words, you'll stick with the Rangers for a while,' chuckled the sheriff. 'Not a bad notion, I'd say. You're doing a heap of good. Well, be seeing you later.'

During the course of the afternoon, Slade visited a number of drinking places. Finally in a little wine room at the edge of town he found Pedro and had a few words with him.

'*Si*, you can find me here when you want me, *Capitan*,' the Mexican youth said. 'A countryman of mine owns this place and has given me work. He and I have already become *amigos*.'

He hesitated a moment, then said, '*Capitan*, something happened this morning that may be of interest to you. Two *señors* came in. One was tall and a very fine looking *señor*. His clothes were the clothes of a *haciendado*— ranch owner—his hair was most black but his face was not, although darkened by wind and sun.'

'What color were his eyes?' Slade instantly asked.

'They were blue,' Pedro replied, 'not the darkly blue that one at times sees in Mexico, but the blue of the ghost flower in the moonlight.'

'Very pale blue,' Slade interpolated.

'*Si*, that is right,' said Pedro. 'The other

señor was very short but with broad shoulders. He wore the, I think you call, business clothes. They sat at table and drank wine and talked. The short *señor* drew much money from his pocket and gave it to the tall one.

' "Here," he said, "is your—" the word I did not know; it sounded like "devay".'

'Divvy,' Slade interpreted.

'*Si*, that is right,' said Pedro. 'The tall *señor* counted the money, and it took long to count. It was not the money of gold, but the money of paper. The short *señor* said, 'Why do you do this? I think it is dangerous.' The tall *señor* said, 'That's my business.' The short *señor* shrugged his shoulders and said no more. They finished their wine and departed.'

Slade sat silent for some moments. Pedro gazed at him expectantly. Finally the Ranger spoke. 'Pedro,' he said, 'what you just told me could be very important. I don't know just how, but it could be. Keep your eyes and ears open and you may learn something else that'll be of value. I'll be seeing you.'

Slade left the little wine room in a very thoughtful mood, for Pedro's description of the tall man who had received the large sum of money was a very fitting description of Craig Telo. And the silver dobe dollars that bulged the pack sacks of the mules of Miguel Allende's smuggler train must have run into a very large sum of money.

A little farther along toward the open

76

country was a hitch rack. Slade paused to lean against it and light a cigarette. He chuckled to himself at Sheriff Wilson's flabbergasted look when he told him of the death of Muerte Blanca more than a year before, the climax of a running gun battle during which Slade had followed the bandit leader across the Rio Grande and far into Mexico. Finally, convinced that his splendid mount could not outrun Shadow, Muerte Blanca had pulled up to shoot it out; but Slade had drawn and killed him before the bandit could pull trigger.

No official report of the affair had ever been made, for Slade had no authority on Mexican soil other than 'holster authority,' which had proved sufficient to terminate the bloody career of the outlaw.

And now some enterprising owlhoot was trading on Muerte Blanca's sinister reputation and cashing in. With authorities in general on the lookout for a hellion with headquarters south of the Rio Grande, which of course is what the outlaw wanted them to do.

All very well, so far as deduction was concerned, but the big question that confronted Slade was—who was the man responsible for the depredations committed in the section during recent months? That he was a shrewd and ruthless operator was beyond argument. The ingenious method which he had used to throw the smuggling train off-guard and the callous killing of the wounded survivor was sufficient proof of both qualities. The raid on the express car, staged almost within sight of town, evinced unusual daring and hinted at little fear of successful pursuit. Which last was something to which Slade gave serious consideration. It predicated a hole-up not far away. One, Slade felt, that could be reached by way of the Smuggler Trail.

His thoughts turned to Craig Telo, the hot-headed spendthrift who had lost the larger portion of his land holding to Rance Horrel. Sheriff Wilson was evidently suspicious of Telo, although Slade did not believe that in his mind he linked Telo with the Muerte Blanca atrocities. He just felt, Slade believed, that there might be something off-color about Telo.

And it appeared the sheriff had reasons on which to base his suspicion. When a man spends more than he seems to have or is able to earn, folks naturally begin wondering where he gets the money.

In fact, Slade was beginning to wonder a little about Telo himself. If Telo was the man who received the money in the wine room—and Slade believed he was—where did that money come from?

Of course, there could be honest explanations. The sale of a herd of cattle or a slice of land, or any other of a number of such things. But why did the transaction take place in the out-of-the-way wine room, and what was the meaning of the short man's remark that the manner in which it was done was dangerous? Two more questions to which Slade didn't have the answers.

However, it appeared there had been no particular attempt at secrecy or the Mexican youth would not have been allowed to witness the transaction.

Struck by a sudden thought, Slade retraced his steps to the wine room, where he found Pedro sweeping the floor. He shot the Ranger an inquiring glance as he entered. Apparently there was nobody else about.

'Pedro,' Slade asked, 'did the two men of whom you spoke know you saw that money passed?'

The Mexican shook his head. 'I would say not, *Capitan*,' he replied. 'I was behind the little partition wall that shuts off the kitchen from the dining room, but I could hear all that was said and I looked through a crack and saw all. I remember that the short *señor* glanced about, as if to make sure they were alone, before he drew the pesos from his pocket.'

'I see,' Slade said. 'Don't talk about it, Pedro, not to anybody.'

'I will not,' the boy promised.

* * *

While Slade was eating a late supper at the Montezuma, Craig Telo and several of his

79

hands entered the saloon. Among them, Slade noted, were the two very short men who looked to be brothers. Recalling Pedro's description of the money passer in the wine room, it looked like Telo made a habit of associating with shorties. And either one of the hammered-down gents, he reflected, could have passed under the wire clothesline that knocked him for a loop the night before.

Telo had a couple of drinks at the bar with his men. Then he sauntered over to a poker game, where it appeared the stakes were rather high, and took a chair. Slade watched him.

Soon Telo's handsome face was flushed, his pale eyes glowing. Has the gambling fever, all right, Slade decided. He continued to watch the game with interest and noted that after a while, Telo several times wrote something on a slip of paper and passed it to the dealer. Each time the dealer motioned to Charley Hansen, the owner of the Montezuma, who entered the back room and a moment later came back with a roll of gold pieces the dealer handed to Telo. The T Bar O owner was evidently losing heavily.

After he finished eating, Slade rose and moved a little closer to the game. Several loiterers were already watching the play and his presence attracted no attention. When a player who sat next to Telo cashed in his chips, Slade stepped forward.

80

'Open game?' he asked casually.

'Always open, if nobody objects,' the dealer answered.

The players, whom Slade judged were ranch or mine owners, looked him over quickly and nodded. Craig Telo flashed a smile that set lights of laughter, rather sardonic laughter, Slade thought, dancing in his pale eyes.

'Don't sit next to me,' he said in a musical voice. 'I'm warning you. The sort of luck I have rubs off on a gent who's too close.'

'Guess I'll risk it,' Slade replied, smiling in turn.

Slade sat down and played for some time with indifferent luck, managing to keep about even. He knew poker and had little fear of getting in too deep. On the other hand, Craig Telo twice had to have his stock of money replenished. However, he did not appear much affected by his losses. Abruptly he shoved back his chair, somewhat to Slade's surprise, for he still had money in front of him and the evening was young.

'They're running against me tonight,' he said with a wry smile. 'I'm going to have a drink and go home.'

'They always run against him,' grunted the dealer as Telo moved away. 'A plunger like him can never win, but he keeps on hoping. Well, guess he can afford it. Reckon his dad left him quite a passel of pesos when he passed on.'

81

Slade nodded and glanced at Telo, who, having downed his drink, was heading for the door, his men trailing behind him.

The dealer was shuffling the slips of paper Telo had signed. He counted them, glanced around, looked under the table.

'I'm short one of these darn I.O.U.s he gave me,' he complained. 'Must have dropped into a spittoon and a swamper packed it off, I reckon. Don't matter. The boss has a check on what he advanced Telo and Craig always pays up just what Hansen says.' He thrust the slips into a drawer and picked up the deck to deal another hand.

Slade played a little longer, then he, too, left the game and the saloon. Five minutes later found him in his room over the stalls, the window of which had been repaired. He drew from his pocket the 'lost' I.O.U., spread it on his knee and placed it beside the crumpled slip of paper he had taken from the body of the dead drygulcher on the slope beyond the canyon where the smugglers were murdered the day before, upon which was noted the advance in wages.

For some moments he studied the two slips. Then he struck a match, touched the flame to Craig Telo's I.O.U. and watched it consumed to ashes. What had looked to be a possible lead had abruptly gone a-glimmering; the two specimens of handwriting were totally different.

Of course a range boss sometimes made out such a memorandum, but under the circumstances that wasn't much help. He restored the first slip to his pocket and went to bed.

CHAPTER TEN

Slade slept fairly late the following morning. After breakfast he visited the sheriff's office and found Wilson in.

'Well, we buried the smugglers,' Wilson said. 'Was Allende's outfit, all right. It was a brutal, ugly business. Smugglers aren't exactly bargains, but, as I said before, they shouldn't be shot down in cold blood. But about that body you said was over the other side of the ridge, you sure you didn't imagine that part of the yarn?'

'Don't think so,' Slade replied. 'Why?'

'Because,' said the sheriff, 'there wasn't anybody there. We searched all over.'

Slade's eyes narrowed slightly. 'Interesting,' he commented, 'and, in my opinion, not exactly bad news.'

'What do you mean by that?' asked the sheriff.

'Well,' Slade explained, 'if you couldn't find the body, it would appear some of the bunch slipped back there and packed it away. Why?

Because they didn't want it brought in and put on exhibition.'

'Meaning that it might have tied up with somebody?'

'So I would presume,' Slade nodded. 'And that leads me to believe what I've already suspected, that some local outfit is mixed up in the deal.'

'But in the name of blazes, who?'

'Easy to ask, hard to answer,' Slade replied.

Sheriff Wilson swore in weary exasperation. 'I sure do wish I'd never given up following a cow's tail,' he declared. 'Have you any notion who it might be?'

Slade shook his head. 'I have nothing on which to base anything concrete,' he answered. 'But I haven't been here long enough to get anything like acquainted with the section and the folks who live here. I've noted one or two things that looked a little queer, but nothing definite enough to even make mention of.'

He paused to roll a cigarette. Abruptly he shot a question at the sheriff. 'How about you, Wilson, have you got anybody in mind?'

The sheriff looked decidedly uncomfortable. 'Well,' he said slowly, 'there's about only one man hereabouts that I know of who makes me wonder just a little.'

'You mean Craig Telo,' Slade stated quietly.

The sheriff jumped a little in his chair. 'I didn't mention Telo,' he protested.

'No, but you were thinking of Telo,' Slade

84

said. 'Well, don't do any thinking out loud. So far as I am able to gather, you have nothing on Telo except that he is a bit wild, a bit reckless and appears to spend more money than he has or earns. All very interesting, but certainly not enough to link a man with cold blooded murder.'

'Do you suspect him at all?' the sheriff asked.

'Wilson,' Slade replied, 'I'm a Ranger, and a Ranger academically suspects anybody who might possibly fit into the picture. That would go for you if I happened to notice something about you that I couldn't explain to my own satisfaction. But that would not mean that I *definitely* suspected you of something off-color. Merely that you were a possibility, and a Ranger does not discard any possibility so long as it remains a possibility. Understand what I mean?'

'Yes, I think I do,' the sheriff said slowly. 'I'll admit I'd hate to think of Craig being mixed up in any skulduggery. I knew his father well and a finer man never lived.'

'Fine fathers don't always have fine sons,' Slade observed, 'so you mustn't allow that to sway you one way or another, any more than it should if a man had a father who was *not* all right. Everyone must be judged on his own merits. And, following the American and the Texan tradition, Craig Telo and everybody else is presumed innocent until proven otherwise.'

'All of which,' said the sheriff, 'seems to get us exactly nowhere.'

'Exactly,' Slade smiled, adding cheerfully, 'but maybe we'll get a break.'

'Or make one,' grunted Wilson. 'I understand El Halcon is pretty good at that.'

'Hope your confidence won't be misplaced,' Slade smiled. 'Well, I'm going out and walk around a while. It's a nice afternoon.'

'Ain't no such thing any more,' grunted the sheriff. 'I got some book work to catch up on. Been on the go so much of late I haven't had much time for the office. I'll be seeing you later, if you drop around.'

'I'll drop in along about dark,' Slade promised.

Slade spent the rest of the afternoon wandering about the town, dropping into various places and listening to the talk. He paid Pedro a visit, but the Mexican boy had nothing new to tell him. After eating his dinner in the Montezuma, he smoked a cigarette or two and watched the dancers on the floor. The sky was scarlet and rose and the blue veil of the twilight was drifting down upon the rangeland when he pinched out the butt of his cigarette, left the saloon and sauntered to the sheriff's office. Wilson was sitting at his desk smoking a black pipe and frowning to himself. He greeted Slade with a nod. The Ranger pulled up a chair and settled himself in

86

a comfortable position.

He didn't stay settled for long, however. He was manufacturing a cigarette in a leisurely fashion when a clatter of hoofs was heard from outside. Glancing out the window he saw a wild-eyed cowhand jerking a lathered horse to a halt.

'Muerte Blanca!' he yelled, leaping to the ground. 'The Livermore stage—they held it up—shot the driver—shot the guard! Got the Borraco Mines payroll. Better'n thirty thousand in gold and silver! Where's the sheriff?'

As Slade and Wilson leaped to their feet, the cowhand came pounding up the steps and into the office, several men who had heard his outburst crowding behind him.

'All right! all right!' bellowed the sheriff. 'Calm down and tell us just what happened. Shut up, you fellers! Give him a chance to talk. All right, son, steady now, take it easy.'

Thus adjured, the cowboy grew calmer. 'I was coming down through the brush from our south pasture,' he explained. 'Heading for the Marathon trail where it forks. I heard shooting and not knowing what it was all about I pulled up and decided I'd better stay where I was till I got the lowdown on what was happening.'

'Lucky you did, or you wouldn't be here telling us about it,' growled the sheriff. 'Go on.'

'In a little bit, a bunch came riding past,' the

cowboy resumed. 'They were wearing black masks except one. He had a white rag tied over his face. Must have been Muerte Blanca. I stayed put till they got out of sight, then I shoved out of the brush and skalleyhooted down the trail. Round a bend I found the stage with the two leaders down. There was a wire stretched across the trail and the leaders fell over it. I got 'em on their feet. The driver was deadhole between his eyes. The guard had both sides of his coat dusted, but he was still living. Managed to tell me what happened before he cashed in. I headed for town fast as my cayuse could go.'

'How many in the bunch?' Slade asked.

'About eight or nine,' replied the puncher. 'I didn't count 'em.'

'And did you notice which way they went?'

'They turned southeast on the Pina Trail,' the hand answered. 'Heading for the Del Nort's, I reckon.'

'Very likely, I'd say,' said Sheriff Wilson. 'Plenty of hole-ups down in those mountains for hellions who know where to find them.' He turned to Slade and said in lower tones, 'This may be the break we were hoping for. Thanks to this feller they didn't count on, they haven't anything like the start they must have figured on, and they're likely to take their time. We should be able to catch 'em up before they get well into the Del Nortes.' He turned to the cowhand.

'Happened about an hour or a little more back?' he asked.

'Just about that,' the other replied. 'I rode fast. Yep, just about an hour, I reckon.'

Sheriff Wilson beckoned the group near the door. 'You fellers scout out and find my three deputies,' he directed. 'Tell them to get a posse together fast as they can. Four or five good men should be enough. You'll find the boys, or one or two of 'em, at the Montezuma eating, I expect. Tell them to shake a leg.'

The men to whom he spoke darted out, the cowboy who had brought the word following them.

'Looks good, don't it?' the sheriff said to Slade.

'Maybe,' the Ranger replied, 'but we're not heading for the Pina Trail.'

Sheriff Wilson stared. 'Why not?' he demanded. 'The feller said they went that way.'

'When he last saw them,' Slade replied. 'But I'm of the opinion they didn't follow the Pina any great distance. Just until they could circle around to the northwest when it began to get dark. Wilson, we're riding for the Smuggler Trail and following it north. I'm playing a hunch, and I believe it's a straight one.'

Sheriff Wilson threw out his hands in a despairing gesture. 'Sounds loco to me,' he declared, 'but whatever you say goes. You can't make a worse hash of it than I've been doing all along. Anyhow, it'll be nice to have somebody to put the blame on. I've been catching a bellyful of that of late.'

'I'll take it, if things don't work out,' Slade grinned. 'But I don't think you'll be telling folks you followed the advice of the notorious El Halcon whom you took along as a special deputy because of what he did at the train wreck.'

The sheriff swore gloomily. 'Guess I'll get it going or coming,' he grumbled. 'Oh, heck! I'm used to it. Here come a couple of the boys now, and with some fellers along. Let's get our horses.'

There were some who stared when the sheriff announced that Slade was going along as a special deputy, but the glances bent on the tall Hawk were distinctly approving.

'Hope you hand it out to 'em the same as you did the other night, feller,' one deputy chuckled.

There were more stares, and some mutters, when Wilson turned into the Smuggler instead of heading due east for the Pina Trail; but the old peace officer was plainly in a very bad temper and the comments were inaudible.

It was Slade who voiced a warning, in a quiet authoritative voice. 'Everybody on their toes every minute,' he said. 'If things work out right, we'll meet the hellions headed this way, and we want to get the jump on them or it's likely to be too bad for us. It's a salty bunch.'

There were nods of agreement.

The night was clear, the sky brilliant with stars. Before they had gone far the moon rose. Objects stood out clear and distinct where the trail was open, but where thick brush encroached upon it the shadows were solid blocks of darkness. The weather had been dry for some time and the trail was fetlock deep in dust and the beat of the horses' hoofs was but a muffled mutter.

Mile after mile they rode, with the moon mounting higher in the sky and the light in the open strengthenings. But directly ahead loomed a long stretch of dense chaparral through which the trail wound and once they entered the brush the gloom was deep, with patches of total blackness where the branches almost interlaced.

Suddenly Slade flung up his head. 'Hold it!' he exclaimed and pulled Shadow to a halt.

And even as the posse jolted to a stop, indistinct figures loomed ahead and to their ears came the soft beat of approaching hoofs.

By a perverse twist of fate the posse had halted where a thin shaft of moonlight streamed down onto the trail. There was a startled shout followed instantly by the blaze of a gun. Slade felt the passing bullet fan his face.

'Let them have it!' he roared, shooting with both hands.

It was a wild and weird battle in the almost

total darkness. Orange flashes split the gloom. The growth quivered to the booming of the guns. Shouts, curses, cries of pain and the neighing of terrified horses rose in a pandemonium of hideous sound. Powder smoke swirled and eddied, its acrid tang stinging the nostrils, blinding the eyes. Possemen and outlaws were shifting shadows blasting death at each other through the murk.

Slade slammed his empty guns into their holsters, jerked his Winchester from the boot and sent Shadow surging ahead. The air was filled with a prodigious crashing as the outlaws took to the brush. Slade heard a whisper of hoofs up the trail. His voice rang out, 'Trail, Shadow! Trail!'

The great black leaped forward, barged head on into two riderless horses. It took Slade moments to untangle him from the furious mixup that followed. Shadow finally freed himself and darted forward. Very quickly they cleared the stand of growth and the open trail lay before them, bathed in the silvery moonlight. And far ahead, fully a thousand yards, a single horseman rode at top speed.

Slade settled himself confidently in the saddle and urged Shadow on, but it soon became apparent that the big black had his work cut out for him. The quarry's horse, a bay or a roan, Slade could not be sure which in the deceptive moonlight, was a splendid animal and his rider knew how to get the most from his mount. Mile after mile sped past, with Shadow very slowly closing the distance. Slade fingered the lock of his rifle but decided the distance was still too great for effective shooting. He urged Shadow to greater efforts.

The black horse responded nobly, snorting, slugging his head above the bit, his glorious dark mane tossing and rippling in the wind of his passing, the moonlight glinting on his foam flecked coat.

'You're doing it, feller,' Slade told him. 'Another hundred yards gained and I'll try a shot at the hellion.' But before Shadow could close the gap that much more, the fugitive suddenly swerved sharply to the right and vanished. Slade muttered an oath and sent Shadow tearing on, his cocked rifle ready for instant action. A few moments more and he saw there was a gap in the straggle of brush that lined the trail. Through it flowed a second and narrower track that trended east by south. Less than a hundred yards from the forks, it swerved around a bend through thicker growth.

Slade sent Shadow charging down the side track. He had almost reached the bend when at the turn a horseman loomed gigantic in the gloom. There was a spurt of reddish flame and the crack of a gun and as Shadow jolted to a halt in obedience to a spasmodic pull on the bridle, the tall form of El Halcon pitched sideways from the saddle and thudded on the dusty trail. A patter of fast hoofs faded away into the silence of the night.

CHAPTER ELEVEN

Slade was unconscious only a few minutes. In fact, he was really not more than half stunned, with all the breath jolted from his body by the fall. He groaned, writhed, flopped over on his side and after a couple of futile attempts managed to assume a sitting position, holding his throbbing head in his hands.

Blood from a shallow gash just above and in front of his left ear trickled over his fingers. He dashed it away petulantly, fumbled out a handkerchief and swabbed the wound, deciding after a brief examination that it was of little consequence. But his head ached and his right hip was badly bruised where it had come in contact with the ground. After a few more minutes of gathering his strength, he got to his feet and limped to where Shadow stood regarding him seriously.

'Well, horse, I fumbled it for fair,' he told the black. 'Barged smack into a trap like a dumb yearling. That was the head man of the bunch, all right, just as I suspected. That hellion seems to specialize in cold nerve and quick thinking. Figured the move he made would throw me off balance for a minute and

I'd head down this snake track after him, never figuring that he'd pull up and wait almost in sight of the main trail. It worked, all right, and if there'd been a mite better shooting light I wouldn't be telling you about it. I should have known better, too, after the one he pulled down by the canyon where he did in the smugglers. Muerte Blanca! Muerte Blanca in his best days wasn't in the class of this sidewinder! Well, I reckon we'd better go back and see how the boys made out with the rest of the devils. Not too good, I'm afraid.'

He retrieved his fallen rifle, made sure it had suffered no damage and that the muzzle was not choked with dust. He sheathed it and with some difficulty, because of his bruised leg, swung into the saddle and returned to the Smuggler Trail.

Slade had not progressed far when he saw a band of horsemen riding swiftly toward him from the south. He cradled the Winchester in the crook of his arm and watched them approach. Soon, however, he recognized the blocky form of Sheriff Wilson in the van.

'Was getting worried about you,' the Sheriff said, as he pulled up beside Slade. 'What happened? There's blood on your face.'

'Outsmarted,' Slade told him briefly. 'The horned toad waited for me at a bend and blew me out of the hull. No, I'm not hurt—just a scratch. How'd you make out?'

'We lost two men,' the sheriff replied

soberly. 'Three more got punctured hides, none serious. We did for five of the devils; the others got away. We tried to chase them through the brush but couldn't come up with them. Got about half of the payroll money back, too. Was in a couple of saddle pouches.'

'Recognize any of the dead men?' Slade asked.

The sheriff shook his head. 'Nobody can recall seeing any of them before,' he replied. 'Ornery looking specimens but about average of what you'd expect. Well, the hellions are getting thinned out a bit, anyhow. Tonight's bag makes eight, including the two you did for at the train wreck and the one down by the canyon we couldn't find.'

'But the head is still mavericking around, and that sort of a head grows a new body in a hurry,' Slade observed. 'If I'd used *my* head a little better tonight, he might be in the bag.'

'Nobody's perfect, not even El Halcon,' the sheriff replied. 'And don't forget, it was you who outsmarted them when you figured they'd head for the Smuggler instead of following the Pina, Trail to the Del Nortes. Otherwise the whole bunch would have gotten in the clear while I was chasing my tail around in circles.'

Slade knew the sheriff meant to be consoling, and there was truth in what he said, but nevertheless Slade was far from satisfied with the night's work and blamed his own lack of foresight for his failure to capture the

96

outlaw chief. Walt Slade was not in the habit of excusing his mistakes, even to himself.

When they reached the scene of the gunfight, the two dead possemen were strapped to their saddles while Slade treated the wounded, none of whom were badly hurt. The slain outlaws' horses had been rounded up and their defunct masters loaded onto them. The grim cavalcade got underway.

Not much speed was made on the return trip to Marta and dawn was streaking the sky with primrose and mauve when they reached town. After routing out the undertaker and disposing of the bodies, Slade went to bed. He was sore all over and his head ached but he had no trouble getting to sleep. Something past noon, he awoke, feeling much refreshed and aside from some stiffness as good as ever.

For some time before arising he lay thinking, reviewing recent incidents and pondering the problem that confronted him.

It was no light problem, he well knew. The man against whom he was pitted was not the conventional type of hole-in-the-wall outlaw of desperate courage, no conscience but elementary mental equipment. That the man posing as Muerte Blanca possessed the former two attributes was self evident; but in addition he certainly did not lack brains. He had a hair-trigger mind that sized up a situation and evaluated it with uncanny speed.

Walt Slade never underestimated an

opponent, which was a cardinal reason for his uniform success against the outlaw fraternity. And in the present instance he had developed a high respect for his adversary. The strategem of sending the horses and mules skalleyhooting on ahead by firing at their heels, so that his followers could creep safely through the brush and retrieve them, out of range of Slade's rifle, evinced ingenuity and resourcefulness; and his lingering behind alone in the hope of getting a shot at the Ranger bespoke cold courage and daring. The estimate was reaffirmed by his act of the night before. He had been willing to take a desperate chance if it afforded an opportunity to down his pursuer. In matching wits with such an individual, Slade knew he had his work cut out for him.

There were plenty of people who maintained that El Halcon had the fastest and most accurate gunhand in Texas. This Slade was very much inclined to doubt. He was fast with a gun, he knew, and had the ability to put his first shot where he aimed, and in a gunfight, the first bullet is very often the conclusive one. But in his opinion there were plenty of men on the other side of the corral fence who were just as good at that sort of thing. His chief advantage lay in his clear, cold mind capable of instantly sizing up a situation, usually correctly, and arriving at split-second decisions. That and an uncanny ability to divine what the other fellow had in mind and to act accordingly. Walt Slade did not outshoot the opposition—although folks who had seen him in action were prone to argue that point—he outthought them.

Of late, however, the luck seemed to have been going a bit bad. Twice it was the other fellow who thought just a bit faster and translated his thought into action. This Slade was willing to concede, and hoped to profit from his mistakes. What lay before him would very likely be a battle of intellects rather than of guns, although there was little doubt but that hot lead would write the final chapter.

But the big question that plagued him was, who the devil was his opponent? The only person he had met so far who seemed to remotely qualify was Craig Telo, but there were flaws in Telo as a suspect that must be given serious thought. So far as Slade had been able to gather, Telo was hot-headed, impulsive, not the type one would expect to coolly analyze a situation before acting. Of course his estimate could be very much wrong. Telo he understood was, like himself, a college man and had shown plenty of ability in managing his extensive properties. Aside from his addiction to gambling, he appeared to be nobody's fool, and the exterior he presented to the public might well be assumed. That there was nothing definite against Telo, Slade was the first to concede, but just the same he felt Craig Telo would bear watching.

With a glance at the sunlight streaming in from the west, he got out of bed, dressed and shaved and went downstairs for a sluice in the trough. He ate a leisurely breakfast at a little restaurant nearby and then repaired to the sheriff's office. Sheriff Wilson greeted him with a scowl.

'Darn you, I don't feel right,' he complained. 'All day folks have been dropping in to congratulate me on the way I handled that business last night and telling me how smart I was to figure those hellions would head back to the Smuggler instead of high-tailing south. I don't like to take credit that isn't due me.'

'Perhaps not,' Slade replied, 'but doing just that at the moment may pay off in the long run. I very much prefer it that way. Be better, I think, if the hellions don't concentrate too strongly on me. Let them watch you and leave me to do a little burrowing underground.'

'Maybe you're right,' the sheriff conceded, 'but I'm getting calluses from pattin' my own back.'

After leaving the office, Slade dropped in at the Montezuma. Standing at the bar was Craig Telo. The rancher waved a cordial greeting.

'My opponent of the other night,' he chuckled. 'Did my bad luck shuck off on you like I figured it would?'

'No,' Slade smiled in reply. 'In fact, I won a few pesos.'

Good for you!' exclaimed Telo. 'I was afraid sitting next to me would put a Comanche cuss on you.'

'I'm afraid you lost a hefty passel,' Slade observed.

Telo shrugged his broad shoulders. 'I usually do,' he admitted, 'but I can afford it. I like to play 'em wild, and you can't win at poker when you play 'em wild. Cards are about my only relaxation—I don't drink much.'

Abruptly his pale eyes danced with laughter. 'Like to see me win?' he asked. 'All right, there's a game over in the corner. Watch me for half an hour if you can spare the time.'

Slade nodded agreement. Telo sat in the game while Slade leaned against a nearby post and watched the play.

From the moment he drew cards, Craig Telo appeared to be a different person. Gone was the reckless plunger who insisted on being in every pot. Replaced by a cold-eyed, steel-nerved, expressionless card sharp who always seemed to do just the right thing, throwing in hands that appeared to be won, the showdown justifying the seemingly senseless thing he did, staying on in a pot against what appeared to be a sure winner across the table, and raking in the chips. Slade could see that he studied every hand played, and the way it was played, and undoubtedly kept track of every card that showed on the table in anticipation of the next deal. The stacks of chips in front of him

101

steadily grew in height.

Telo glanced up, caught Slade's eye and again his own danced with laughter. Abruptly he cashed in his chips, took Slade by the arm and returned to the bar.

'But it isn't fun that way,' he complained. 'Might as well be digging postholes or branding calf critters. I just wanted to show you I'm not exactly the darn fool you figured me to be. As I said, I can afford to lose what I lose, and if I really want to win, I can win. I mavericked around quite a bit before Dad died and I didn't have the responsibility of the spread on my shoulders. Was over East and lots of places and did lots of things. Spent one whole summer dealing on a Mississippi River steamboat, and when you deal on one of those boats, you learn about all there is to learn about cards. Well, be seeing you. I got some chores to attend to.' With a smile and a nod he finished his drink and strolled out.

Slade watched him go, the concentration furrow deep between his black brows. He was drastically revising his estimate of Craig Telo.

CHAPTER TWELVE

A little later Slade left the saloon. As he sauntered along he noticed men going in and out of the undertaking establishment, which was a little farther down the street and on the opposite side. He crossed the street and entered the parlor. Don Hobart, the undertaker, and several men were standing around talking, among them was Sheriff Wilson. Slade glanced at the bodies of the outlaws laid out for inspection. Those of the two slain possemen were decently coffined in an other room.

Sheriff Wilson nodded to Slade and after finishing his conversation with the man with whom he was speaking joined the Ranger.

'Let's walk up to the office,' he suggested. Slade was agreeable to the suggestion and they left the parlor. When they reached the office Wilson sat down at his desk and began filling his pipe. Slade rolled a cigarette.

'Well,' he asked, 'were any of them recognized?'

Sheriff Wilson gazed at him with a slightly queer expression, Slade thought.

'Yes,' he said slowly, 'one of them was recognized.' He paused to light his pipe. Slade waited expectantly.

'Yes, one was recognized,' the sheriff repeated. 'Several people recalled that the chunky one with the red mark on his cheek, sort of a birthmark, used to ride for Craig Telo. I thought so last night but wasn't plumb sure, so I didn't say anything. Yes, he worked for Craig, all right.'

The sheriff paused again, fussing with his

pipe, and Slade remained silent, confident that there was more to come.

'I hunted up Craig—he's in town today—and took him to Hobart's place,' the sheriff resumed. 'He didn't argue the point when he looked at the jigger. Said sure he'd worked for him, several months back. Said he'd fired him when he caught him snooping around in the room he uses for an office and going through some of his private papers. Said he kicked him out and gave him his time and that he hadn't seen him from that day to this. Come to think of it, nobody else could recall seeing the devil for several months. That much of his story was corroborated, anyhow.'

Slade puffed on his cigarette in silence for some little while. The sheriff watched him.

'So it doesn't mean much,' Slade commented at length. 'That is aside from the coincidence that one of the robbers worked for Telo, the man you've been looking at sort of sideways. According to all the evidence, Telo hasn't been associating with him of late. Interesting that nobody has seen him since he worked for Telo, but he was still hanging around the section. What is really important, if we could learn it, is where did he hole up in the meantime? Of course he could have left the section after Telo fired him and then returned, but that seems a bit farfetched. Did you get a chance to interview any of Telo's hands?'

'A couple,' replied the sheriff. 'They remembered the horned toad, all right. Said he wasn't overly liked when he was with the T Bar O, although he was a good worker. Said he kept to himself and didn't associate with the other boys when he didn't have to. Sulky sort, I gather. Bill Cowdry, one of the hands, said Craig hired him because he looked pretty seedy when he showed up at the spread and told Craig he'd been sick. Bill 'lows that Craig will always fall for that sort of a yarn. Anyhow, he signed him on.'

'Cowdry know why Telo fired him?' Slade asked.

'Oh, sure,' said the sheriff. 'He gave the same reason Craig did. He said that in his opinion the sidewinder had an eye on the office safe, where Craig always keeps considerable money, according to Cowdry. Craig didn't say anything about the safe.'

'Considering the circumstances under which he was gathered in, it appears quite possible Cowdry was right,' Slade observed.

'If Telo really did honestly fire him,' the sheriff remarked with a grunt.

'There appears to be no evidence that he did not,' Slade pointed out.

Wilson's only answer was another grunt. Slade did not pursue the discussion. The sheriff was prejudiced against Craig Telo and argument wouldn't change him.

'Well, we appear to be getting nowhere

fast,' he remarked. 'Perhaps we're making a mistake by concentrating on local residents. This town is a stopping-off place for passing-through gents, I gather.'

'It's that, all right,' the sheriff agreed morosely.

'But that missing body by the canyon where the smugglers were murdered, that can't be dismissed,' Slade observed. 'Why would an outside bunch spirit it away? I'd like to have the answer to that one.'

'You answer it,' growled Wilson. 'You're the Ranger. I'm just a poor old sheriff, trying to get along.'

'You're not doing so bad,' Slade chuckled. 'Anything else interesting happen since last night?'

'Nothing except Rance Horrel came in to say he's still losing cows,' the sheriff replied. 'He brought along another itemized list.'

'Meticulous sort of gent,' Slade remarked. 'Well, that kind is usually a good businessman, keeping a finger on everything. The trouble with too many cattlemen is that they're slovenly in business matters. Safe to say Horrel hasn't any unbranded mavericks roaming around. Horrel! Wonder if he's any relation to the bunch by that name of Lampasas County, who had the feud with the Higginses?'

'I doubt it,' said the sheriff. 'He spells his name with one L while the Horrells of Lampasas County used two, and I don't recall

106

any of 'em having the first name of Rance. Although one of the bunch was said to have escaped when the other five brothers were taken from the Bosque County jail and lynched by the mob. Some argument about that. All six were supposed to be prime attractions at the necktie party, but there are folks who say that one escaped. They were a salty bunch, all right. Nope, I doubt if our specimen belonged to that outfit. The Horrells were good cattlemen, though, and would have done all right if they hadn't gotten mixed up with Pink Higgins and his bunch. That was the beginning of their trouble. Then they just about exterminated a bunch of state police, a very unpopular outfit, and moved to Lincoln County, New Mexico. Should have stayed there. Came back to Texas, got thrown in jail by Lieutenant Reynolds of the Rangers, were released and later rearrested and locked up again. That was the finish of them. They'd been put in charge of county officials who didn't resist the mob.'

'An interesting chapter in the history of Texas range wars,' Slade observed. 'If one did escape, he'd be pretty well along in years now.'

'If it was the youngest, who wasn't much more than a kid at the time, he'd be in his forties, I reckon,' said the sheriff. He twinkled his eyes at Slade. 'About the age of our Horrel,' he added.

Slade laughed. 'Would be something in the

107

nature of coincidence if our Horrel was the missing brother,' he commented, 'and it wouldn't mean a thing if it was so. Any lawbreaking the Horrells might have been mixed up in was forgotten long ago, and if one managed to escape the lynching and made good in another section, I'd say it's to his credit.'

'You've got the right of it there,' agreed the sheriff. 'Anyhow we've got troubles of our own without digging up old ones that happened more than twenty years back.'

Slade continued his stroll in a disgruntled frame of mind. All very well to look on Craig Telo as a prime potential suspect but the cold facts of the case were that there was absolutely nothing definite on which to base a suspicion that Telo was mixed up in wrongdoing. It appeared he received money from mysterious sources, and it was established that one of the stage robbers had once worked for him. Which fact Telo readily admitted and added information that merely corroborated the already accepted fact that the hellion was an unsavory character. A man could not be condemned for hiring a hand, apparently out of commiseration more than anything else, who later turned out to be unworthy of consideration. The afternoon poker game had heightened Slade's estimate of Telo's intelligence, but there was nothing unusual about a man who could afford the game playing recklessly because he derived pleasure from so doing. Such a procedure was common in a low-stake game and low-stake games were merely a matter of relativity. A ten-dollar limit was no different from a ten-cent limit except in the amount the individual players could afford to lose.

So, all in all, he didn't have a darn thing on Telo, or anybody else, for that matter.

Slade spent the rest of the evening wandering about aimlessly, trying to evaluate what he had learned and correlate it with previous happenings, with little success. As dusk was falling, he turned into the Root Hog, smaller than the Montezuma but even livelier. Standing at the bar was Rance Horrel conversing pleasantly with a bartender. Slade watched him idly, thinking that he was certainly a fine-looking man. He was toying with a filled glass and still regarding Horrel when Craig Telo pushed through the swinging doors. His face was flushed and Slade had a notion he had been drinking. He passed by without, apparently, seeing the Ranger, his eyes, hot and glittering, fixed on Rance Horrel. As he reached Horrel he paused and said something Slade could not quite catch. Horrel instantly replied and again Slade could not quite catch what was said.

Whatever it was, it appeared to infuriate the T Bar O owner. His face whitened and his hand streaked to his gun.

He was fast, but before he cleared leather he was looking into a black muzzle. Rance Horrel spoke, his voice quiet but in the depths of his pale eyes a flicker like to flames.

'Telo,' he said, 'I don't want to kill you, but if you keep acting up you'll make me.'

Craig Telo stood perfectly motionless, regarding him. His face showed no fear, only intense calculation. The look, Slade thought, of a man who has unexpectedly encountered something that holds latent possibilities.

'There are other things beside a fast gunhand, Horrel,' he said softly, turned and left the saloon.

Slade glanced at Rance Horrel. He wasn't smiling and on his face was a look of malignant hatred as his eyes followed Telo out the door.

It was gone in an instant, however. He smiled, shrugged his shoulders, holstered his gun and raised his glass with a steady hand.

'Brother! I thought Craig Telo was due for his come-uppance,' a bartender mumbled over Slade's shoulder. 'Reckon Horrel would have got his, too, though. I figure Craig would have pulled that gun and shot even if he had a slug through his heart; he's that sort. Here, feller, have a snort with me, I'm shaking like quince jelly in a thunderstorm!'

Slade chuckled and raised the glass the barkeep had filled sloppily. The drink juggler stared enviously at the brimming glass that did not spill a drop.

'Reckon you ain't got no nerves at all!' he grumbled. 'Have another one.'

CHAPTER THIRTEEN

Slade finished his drink, thanked the friendly bartender and left the Root Hog. He hesitated a moment, then turned his steps to the Montezuma farther up the street. He figured Craig Telo would be there.

He was, sitting at a table with a glass in front of him. He caught Slade's eye and gestured to a vacant chair.

'Reckon you saw it, eh?' he asked as Slade sat down.

The Ranger nodded.

'I shouldn't have said to him what I did,' Telo remarked.

'What did you say?' Slade asked curiously.

'I said, "Hello, thief!"'

'Not a nice thing to say, unless you have proof that he is one,' Slade reprimanded 'What did he say to you?'

'He said, '"A skunk can't smell his own odor!"'

Slade chuckled. 'Rather a neat repartee,' he observed.

Telo smiled wryly. 'It was,' he admitted, 'and riled me enough to cause me to make a fool of myself. Fast, wasn't he?'

'Very,' Slade conceded. He indicated the Colt at Telo's hip. 'You'd be better off without that gun,' he said.

'Why?' Telo asked.

'Because you're no quick-draw man. You don't wear your iron right, and you don't hold your hands right. And if you keep on reaching when you're riled, it's going to get you killed.'

'I guess you're right,' Telo agreed soberly. 'I'm darn good with a rifle, but I never seemed able to properly get the hang of a six.'

'Stick to a rifle,' Slade advised, adding, 'and be slow to use that; a dead man doesn't make a soft pillow at night.'

'I guess you know,' Telo observed.

'I do,' Slade said shortly. He paused, then asked, 'What's the trouble between you and Horrel?' He wanted to hear Telo's version of the affair.

Telo proceeded to tell him, and the story basically agreed with what Slade had already heard.

'And you do not consider Horrel's claim valid?' he asked when Telo stopped talking.

'I know it's not,' the rancher replied.

'How about your grandfather's signature on the deed to the Spanish soldier of fortune?'

'It appears authentic,' Telo admitted. 'Anyhow, Horrel's lawyer and a handwriting expert agreed that it is. How it got on that old paper I don't know, but I do know my grandfather never deeded that land to anybody. If he had, my father would have known about it, and he would have told me.'

'Men sometimes slip up in such matters, or forget,' Slade reminded.

'I'll agree with you there,' Telo replied, 'and if it were not for certain peculiar circumstances, I'd be inclined to admit that such might have been the case.' He paused again, eyeing Slade contemplatively, appeared to make up his mind to something.

'I'm going to tell you something else, in strictest confidence,' he announced. He glanced at Slade inquiringly. The Ranger nodded.

'Reckon that's more than another man's bond,' Telo said, 'so here goes. First I'll preface what I'm going to tell you by saying I don't need that land. I didn't need it much before Horrel got his claws on it, and I certainly don't now. That portion of the land was occupied by small farmers and ranchers, and when Horrel got possession, he booted them all off. I managed to place most of them elsewhere, but the land was home to them and it broke their hearts to leave it. That's why I see red every time I think of Horrel.

'And because of those tenants, I know that Grandfather Telo never deeded that land to anybody,' he said impressively.

'Why?' Slade asked, although he was beginning to vaguely guess what was coming.

'Because Grandfather Telo settled them on

113

that land,' Telo answered. 'Or rather, he settled their fathers or grandfathers on it. They were old friends and acquaintances he brought up from Mexico because he wanted them to have homes in a free country. He would never have sold the land from under them. One of his last commendations to my father, shortly before he died, which I happened to overhear, was that the tenants should never be deprived of their land and that my father should safeguard their interests in every way, they being mostly ignorant people.'

'And he was of sound mind at the time and before his death? Did not suffer from senility?'

'Spry as a cricket and handled the affairs of the ranch right up to the day of his death,' Telo replied. 'Just went to sleep one night and didn't wake up, as old men sometimes do-the lucky ones.'

'I see,' Slade said thoughtfully.

'And now,' resumed Telo, 'I'll finish the yarn and show you why I don't need that land for myself. When he was alive, Dad did a lot of speculating in land in other sections of the state. Did pretty well, too. Buy, hold a while, and sell at a profit. But with one parcel down in the Neuces country he appeared to have gotten stuck. Shortly after he acquired it they had one drought year after another in that section and folks began moving out, and of course, the value of the land went down to almost nothing. But Dad always kept the taxes

114

paid up, and so did I.'

Telo paused to beckon a waiter to refill their glasses and then resumed. 'Remember the big oil strike in the Neuces country a few years back?' he asked. Slade nodded.

'Well,' Telo said, 'the holding I'm speaking of is in that particular section. 'About a year ago an oil company approached me and wanted to drill on the land. I had no objections and an agreement was signed. The first well they put down came in a gusher, and so did the next and the next. A dozen of 'em going now and all producing. I'm making more money than I ever dreamed of making. And that's the part of the story I most especially don't want repeated. Nobody in the section knows about it and it's driving a good many of them loco trying to figure where I get the money I spend, and throw away gambling. I have my dividends sent to me personally by messenger, in cash, never by check or to the local bank.'

'Why in the devil do you do such a loco thing?' Slade wondered.

'Oh, just to keep the busybodies guessing,' Telo returned with a grin, 'especially those who sided with Horrel in the row. I tell you if they don't get the lowdown soon, some of them are going to pass out by way of apoplexy or some other kind of a stroke.'

Slade shook his head at this manifestation of malicious humor. 'And what do you do with the surplus that must keep piling up?' he asked.

'Keep it in the big safe at the ranch house,' Telo replied. 'It's pretty well stuffed.'

Slade whistled under his breath. 'And did you ever stop to think you're just naturally asking for trouble by keeping such a large sum on your property?'

'Oh, nobody knows about it but my range boss, Zeke Sutton, and I'd trust Zeke with my life,' Telo replied lightly.

And that was just what Telo was doing, Slade reflected grimly, trusting Zeke Sutton with his life.

Telo was regarding him curiously. 'I wonder why the devil I told you all this?' he said. 'There seems to be something about you that makes a man want to talk to you, and spill his guts.'

Telo didn't know it, but others had remarked on this peculiar quality of Walt Slade's.

'Sometimes does a man good to talk,' Slade replied, 'and you can rely that it won't go any further. And for the love of Pete, don't tell anybody else about that money you have stashed in your ranch house. My advice is to pack it to the bank and put it where it will be safe, and you safer in consequence.'

'Perhaps I will,' Telo said. 'Maybe I'm carrying a joke a bit too far.'

'You certainly are, for your own good,' Slade declared emphatically.

Telo nodded and stood up. 'I'm going

home,' he announced. He hesitated a moment. 'And I really think I'll take your advice, about the money.'

'Do that,' Slade replied, 'and don't put it off. You're playing with dynamite to gratify a bizarre whim, and the satisfaction you get from teasing your neighbors I don't consider adequate compensation for the risk you're taking.'

Telo nodded again, and regarded him speculatively for a moment. 'Slade,' he said, 'you have a rather remarkable vocabulary for a wandering cowhand, or an—'

'An outlaw,' Slade finished smilingly.

'For an outlaw,' Telo repeated with a grin. 'So long!'

He walked out, jauntily, evidently in a much better temper than when Slade entered. The Ranger watched him go, and once again the concentration furrow was deep between his black brows.

He was doing some hard thinking, and he was in an unenviable frame of mind; things were getting more scrambled by the minute. Telo's story had bordered on the fantastic, but Slade was forced to admit it had the ring of truth. And if it wasn't true, why should Telo concoct such an outlandish yarn that a little quiet investigation would prove false if it was false? The answer to that Slade considered of deep personal interest to himself. If Telo had deliberately lied, manufacturing the tale from

117

the whole cloth, he must have had a motive for doing so. And the motive? Well, Slade could figure one without much difficulty.

The whole thing might be a cunningly conceived trap. Telo knew him for El Halcon, of course, and was very likely familiar with the myth that had grown up around El Halcon, his reputation for horning in on other people's good things and skimming off the cream. If Telo was mixed up in something off-color, he might believe that Slade was in the section for just that purpose and be determined to forestall any attempt on El Halcon's part to take over the exceedingly lucrative outlaw operations that had been active for some time. The very large sum of money he claimed reposed in his ranch house safe would be a temptation to any owlhoot and might well be the bait. Perhaps, he reasoned, El Halcon would make a try for the money, and if he did so, the jaws of the trap would close and the pest that was El Halcon would be eliminated once and for all.

Nothing but conjecture, of course, but at the moment conjecture was all he had to go on . . .

He wondered if Telo had recognized him as a Ranger, but didn't think so. Telo would know very well that a Ranger would be apt to check his story and if it was false, quickly disprove it. In fact, Slade intended to do a little checking, in his own way.

But if Telo's story was authentic as to detail,

it abruptly placed Rance Horrel in a rather peculiar position. It did not appear reasonable that old Manuel Telo, who stood in the nature of a *patron* to his tenants, would have deeded away the land they occupied. An honorable Mexican *patron*—and nothing warranted the presumption that Manuel Telo had been other than honorable—regards himself as the father of a family of which his tenants are the members. He would not dream of knowingly doing anything that might jeopardize their interests or work to their disadvantage. Land frauds were not uncommon in the Southwest, especially where old Spanish grants and deeds were concerned. The Telo-Horrel controversy could be a shrewdly conceived example.

However, that was an extraneous matter and of little interest to Slade. He was not in the section to expose swindles but to run down and eliminate a gang of murderous outlaws. Telo and Horrel could settle their differences in the courts, where doubtless a just decision would be arrived at.

Anyhow, no matter how you looked at it, the whole business was a mess. Craig Telo, so far as surface indications went, at least, seemed to be easing himself out of the role of a suspect. And if Telo was to be eliminated as a suspect, who the devil was he to look to? Slade didn't know and decided to call it a day and go to bed. The bullet cut on the side of his head was already healing nicely, but his bruised hip was still sore and stiff.

Ever since the attack on him by gun and dynamite, he approached the stable warily. Nothing happened and ten minutes later he was sound asleep.

CHAPTER FOURTEEN

Slade awoke early. He ate breakfast then got the rig on Shadow and rode south by way of the old Smuggler Trail. He did not follow the trail for any great distance; a couple of miles south of the forks he turned to the right and left the beaten track.

Something like a half mile to the west was a range of low hills, little more than magnified rises, that trended steadily south for as far as the eye could reach. They were heavily brush grown and a rider following their contours would be pretty well shielded from the gaze of anybody traveling the Smuggler. He made for the hills and discovered it would not be difficult to follow their lower slopes. Threading his way through the growth he rode steadily south. After a while he passed the Telo ranch house, its gray walls softened and mellowed by the golden morning sunshine. He continued on his way and later passed the smaller building that was Rance Horrel's RH *casa*. He noted with interest that the bunk house was set a good two hundred yards from the main building, with a grove between.

Still he did not pause, but continued on his way for several miles more, until the RH ranch house was well behind. Then he turned Shadow and rode east to the Smuggler. On the far side of the trail the land rolled upward in a gentle slope to the rounded crest of a rise. Slade sent Shadow up the slope to its summit, where he reined in and sat gazing across the prospect ahead.

Below the rise crest, the country lay spread before his eyes like a map, mile on mile of excellent rangeland stretching to the thin, fine line of the horizon. And dotting the level pastures and set fairly well apart were a number of small ranch houses, all built in the Mexican style. There were also clusters of adobes, very old in appearance, some with roof and walls intact, others in ruins. Slade rode on down the far slope and approached one of the scattering of little houses built of sun-dried brick. He saw that once fences had surrounded patches of land, but the posts had been uprooted, the wire removed. Slade considered the dreary prospect with serious eyes. Here, to an extent at least, was corroboration of Craig Telo's story. Beyond question the land had been occupied by small ranchers and peon farmers who had been evicted from their humble homes no great while before.

For some little time he rode about among

these sad mementoes of onetime happiness and content. Then he breasted the slope and sent Shadow on across the Smuggler to the brush-grown hills beyond. In the outer fringe of growth he pulled up, rolled a cigarette and with one long leg hooked comfortably over the saddle horn smoked thoughtfully.

'Horse,' he told Shadow, 'I've got a hunch. Not much of a hunch, just a little hazy one, but I figure to play it. That is if I can figure a way to play it. A mighty slim hunch, but it might work.'

Shadow rolled his eyes and snorted resignedly, as much as to say, 'Here we go again!' Slade chuckled, pinched out his butt and settled his feet in the stirrups.

'Might as well head back to town,' he observed and rode north, still keeping to the fringe of brush. 'Be easier going on the trail over there but I don't want to be seen snooping around down here, at least not yet,' he explained to his mount.

When he came abreast of the T Bar O ranch house on the far side of the trail, some time later, he saw a man riding down the driveway from the *casa* to turn north. The distance was not too great to recognize Craig Telo, who was apparently heading for town. Slade, riding parallel to the trail, watched him for some time. Telo rode steadily at a fair pace, never looking back. Slade finally decided to join the rancher; he wanted a few words with Telo.

Where Telo rode at the moment the trail was open, but not far ahead it was lined on either side by a stand of growth that extended for some miles. It was not very heavy growth and Slade knew Shadow would have no difficulty making his way through it. He veered a little and took a diagonal course across the prairie that would bring him to the trail some distance ahead of where Telo had vanished between the rows of chaparral. He quickened Shadow's pace and soon the big black was threading his way between the tree trunks. Another few minutes and through a final straggle, Slade sighted Telo. The ground was covered deep with dead leaves and Shadow's hoofs made but a whisper of sound that apparently did not reach Telo's ears, for he did not turn his head.

Slade was less than a score of yards distant and was about to raise his voice in a shout when a shot rang out from the brush on the far side of the trail. Craig Telo gave a sharp cry, clapped his hand to his left breast, reeled in the saddle and fell.

From the brush dashed two masked men who made straight for Telo's riderless horse.

Slade jerked his guns and sent Shadow charging forward. The pair whirled at the sound of hoofbeats. Slade caught a gleam of metal and fired pointblank, again and again.

One of the drygulchers went down to lie in a motionless, huddled heap. The other dodged behind Telo's horse and fired at Slade. The Ranger shot back, the slug tearing the pommel from Telo's saddle. He felt the wind of a passing bullet, threw down on the almost invisible outlaw and pulled trigger as Shadow's hoofs clanged on the surface of the trail.

A hat sailed through the air. Its owner yelled a curse, dived across the trail and slid into the growth like a snake, Slade blasting lead after him. A moment later there was a prodigious crashing in the brush and the pound of hoofs. Slade's hand tightened on the bridle, he glanced at Telo, who was writhing and groaning on the ground, and gave up any idea of pursuing the fleeing drygulcher. Telo appeared to be hard hit and even a few minutes neglect might cost his life. Slade slid from the saddle and knelt beside him.

'Easy! easy!' he told the wounded man. 'Keep still and let me see how much damage is done.'

Telo obeyed, gasping. Slade saw the whole front of his shirt was dyed with blood. With his knife he cut away the drenched cloth and laid bare the wound, breathing a sigh of relief.

'Take it easy,' he repeated. 'It isn't so bad. Slug went through the flesh just under your shoulder. Two inches to the right and you'd have been a goner, but I think I can patch this up okay. Lie still, now.'

He secured bandage and salve from his saddle pouches, padded the wound to control the flow of blood and deftly bandaged it. For a few moments he watched the lessening amount of stain on the white cloth and nodded with satisfaction.

'Feeling better?' he asked.

'A lot,' Telo replied.

Slade rolled and lighted a cigarette and placed it between Telo's lips. 'Lie right there where you are till you smoke that,' he directed. 'That hunk of lead hit you a devil of a wallop in a sensitive spot and I think you're suffering from shock more than anything else; you didn't have time to lose much blood.'

'Did you get the devils?' Telo asked, between drags on the cigarette.

'One of them,' Slade answered, glancing at the huddled form nearby. 'The other got away. I was afraid to take time to run him down. Guess it's just as well I didn't. You might have lost enough blood to badly weaken you.'

Squatting on his heels, he rolled a cigarette for himself, lighted it and regarded the rancher through the blue mist of the smoke.

'Telo,' he said abruptly, 'what the devil is this all about?'

Craig Telo hesitated, then waved his good hand toward his horse.

'There's close to seventy thousand dollars in those saddle pouches,' he replied. 'I was taking your advice and packing it to the bank.'

'I see,' Slade said thoughtfully. 'Who knew you were taking that money to the bank?'

'Only Zeke Sutton, my range boss,' Telo answered. 'He wanted to ride with me but I told him it wasn't necessary. Looks like maybe he was right.'

'Judging from recent happenings, apparently he was,' Slade commented dryly. Privately he wondered just how justified was Telo's faith in Zeke Sutton. Through his mind flitted a vision of the wage memorandum he took from the pocket of the dead smuggler killer, the memorandum that *could* have been signed by a range boss.

'Think you can sit up now?' he asked as Telo finished his smoke.

'Sure,' the other replied. With Slade's assistance he did. He sat for a few minutes, then asked to be helped to his feet. Once erect, he weaved a little but soon stood firm.

'Now I'll have a look at that sidewinder I bagged,' Slade said. He turned the body over on its back and ripped off the black mask, revealing a lean, saturnine face with little outstanding about it. Craig Telo uttered a sharp exclamation.

'Slade, that fellow used to work for me!'

'The devil he did!'

'Yes, he did,' Telo repeated.

'And did you fire him?' Slade asked, thinking of the dead train wrecker Telo had said he fired.

Telo shook his head. 'No, he quit a couple of weeks back. Said he was going over east where he had folks. I hadn't seen him from that day to this.' He repeated Slade's question of a few minutes before, 'What the devil does this mean?'

'It means, perhaps among other things, that you've been using bad hiring judgment, I'd say,' Slade replied. He knelt beside the body and deftly emptied the dead man's pockets, revealing considerable money, but nothing else of significance. His clothes were regulation rangeland variety, his fallen gun a standard Colt Forty-five.

'Never anything to tie the hellions up with somebody,' Slade observed. 'Maybe his horse is back in the brush and might tell us something, if it didn't take off when the other sifted sand. I'll see.'

However, a search of the brush revealed no trace of the animal. Slade returned to the trail, where Telo was leaning against his horse and puffing another cigarette.

'Must have followed the other one,' he told the rancher. 'Telo, have you more new hands working for you at present?'

'Yes, several,' Telo admitted. 'There's a good deal of a labor turnover in this section. I have a core of old-timers who stick with me, but somebody is always quitting and somebody being hired to take his place. Why?'

'Because there's little doubt that somebody learned you planned to take the money to the bank today and passed the word along,' Slade explained. 'When did you and Sutton discuss the matter?'

'Last night.'

'Where?'

'In the ranch house living room.'

'With the windows open?'

'Yes.'

'And evidently the wrong pair of ears was listening,' Slade said.

'It looks that way,' Telo agreed. 'It also looks like I'm pretty heavily in your debt. I'm of the opinion that not only would I have lost the money, but very likely my life as well. Chances are I'd have bled to death if I was left alone on the trail. And in line with what has happened in this section recently, there's a great likelihood that those devils would have decided against leaving a possible witness alive.'

'Appears to be standard procedure hereabouts,' Slade conceded.

'So—' Telo half turned to one of the saddle pouches, met Slade's smiling gaze and flushed a little. 'So I'm saying thank you, one devil of a lot!' he concluded.

Slade nodded and deftly changed the subject. 'Think you're able to ride?' he asked.

'Give me a boost into the hull and I'll be okay,' Telo answered. A moment later he had his feet in the stirrups.

'Feel a bit shaky, but I'll make it,' he said.

'Best if you can,' Slade said as he forked

Shadow. 'I think you're all right, but I want the doctor to have a look at you as quickly as possible. Also,' he added with a smile, 'I'll feel easier when that dinero is safe in the bank. That's a lot of pesos to be riding herd on, especially in a section like this. Let's go. We'll leave that carcass lying and the sheriff can ride down and bring it in.'

They reached Marta without further untoward event and stopped first at the doctor's office. Slade stood by the window and kept an eye on the saddle pouches while the old practitioner looked Telo over.

'Not much left for the doctor after Slade works on a jigger,' he observed. 'He either leaves him finished business for the undertaker or on the road to recovery.'

Telo chuckled weakly, understanding without difficulty what the doctor meant.

'Come on, Slade, let's go to the bank,' he suggested, 'and then across the street to the Montezuma for a snort. Be all right, won't it, Doc?'

'Sure,' the doctor replied, 'that is if you don't put away enough to cause you to fall down and start that hole bleeding again.'

At the bank, the receiving teller gasped and goggled as Telo silently shoved the thick packets of big bills across the counter. Slade could see that he was bursting with questions that professional ethics didn't allow him to ask. Telo accepted his deposit slip, nodded and still

129

not speaking walked out with Slade, the bank employees staring after him. Outside he chuckled again, with unholy glee.

'That jigger just about busted a blood vessel,' he chortled. 'Although they're not supposed to do it, somebody will spill the beans sure as shooting and the word will be all over town before dark. Sheriff Wilson will be sending wires to every bank in the county to find out which one has been robbed recently. Craig Telo and El Halcon! Hope he doesn't throw us in the calaboose on general principles.'

'I doubt if he will,' Slade smiled. 'Let's go get that snort and then something to eat. I'm hungry enough to put away a barbecued steer and you need something to make up for the blood you lost.'

Telo's bandaged shoulder had been noticed as they rode into town and at the Montezuma they were quickly surrounded by a questioning crowd. Telo related what happened, and the story lost nothing in the telling, especially the part Slade played.

''Pears nobody is safe any more,' old John Archibald who owned the big Swinging J declared wrathfully. 'That is,' he added, shooting an admiring glance at Slade, 'unless he has this young feller for a bodyguard. Son, you've done more to clean up this section since you've been here than all the sheriffs and deputies we've had in the past five years. You

130

ought to be with the Rangers!'

There was a general nodding of agreement.

CHAPTER FIFTEEN

Later in the evening, after Telo had hired a room and lain down to rest, Slade visited the sheriff's office.

'Yes, I heard about it,' Wilson said. 'Guess everybody in town has, and somebody at the bank blabbed, too. Slade, where the devil did Craig Telo get all that money?'

'From a legitimate business investment,' Slade replied. 'Wilson, you might as well lay off Telo. He's not our man.'

The sheriff stared. 'The devil you say!'

Slade nodded. 'I'm convinced he's not,' he repeated. 'In fact, been dubious about him from the very beginning.'

'Why?' asked the sheriff.

'Because he was too darn obvious,' Slade explained. 'Right from the start he appeared to fill all the requirements of the ideal suspect, and I've learned from experience, sometimes unpleasant, that the ideal suspect is seldom the right one. I'll admit he had me puzzled, and for a while I leaned toward him as the man we wanted. One thing after another appeared to point the finger of suspicion at Telo and I mistakenly concentrated on him. If I hadn't, a

131

couple of men might not have died and the Borraco Mines wouldn't have lost half their payroll. An inexcusable blunder, but there's no use crying over spilt milk.'

'I never yet heard of a gent who was infallible,' said the sheriff. 'And I don't think you're justified in blaming yourself for what very likely would have happened in any event.'

'Perhaps not,' Slade conceded. 'Anyhow I take a certain consolation from the fact that, in my opinion, I've run up against a man smarter than myself; he's a shrewd character, all right.

'But,' he added reflectively, 'I've noticed that his sort always has a weakness through which he can be reached. The myth of Achilles has never been improved on. When Achilles' mother dipped him in the waters of the River Styx, thereby rendering him invulnerable to all mortal weapons, she held him by one heel, and that heel was not submerged and remained mortal. That was the weakness of Achilles and rendered him vulnerable to the arrow of Paris, which struck him in the heel and finished him. Yes, an off-color individual always has a weakness which, sooner or later, is the cause of his downfall. Isn't very hard to see the finger of Providence in such matters; otherwise some ruthless scoundrel might well upset the existing order of things and change the destiny of mankind. But when any man opposes himself against the eternal Law, sooner or later he is hurled back by it and broken.'

'A bit hard to follow you, but I figure I sort of get what you mean,' said the sheriff. 'And what's the particular weakness of the gent in question?'

'Greed,' Slade replied. 'He's in the same category as a big pig who shoves all the little pigs aside, deprives them of their small share and turns over the trough. That act on his part opened up an avenue of speculation that may prove to be his downfall, if the hunch I'm playing turns out to be a straight one.'

He paused to roll a cigarette, his eyes dark with thought. Sheriff Wilson waited expectantly.

'Wilson,' Slade said suddenly, 'I want to look at all the papers dealing with the Telo-Horrel land controversy. I understand they are at the courthouse here.'

Sheriff Wilson was no fool, and he could see as far into the trunk of a tree as most.

'So Rance Horrel is the man you have in mind, eh?' he remarked.

'He is,' Slade conceded, adding, 'but remember, there is not one scintilla of evidence linking Horrel with wrong doing. And unless I can definitely prove to my own satisfaction that he is mixed up in something off-color, I hesitate to even trust my intuition in the matter.'

Sheriff Wilson shook his head. 'I'm afraid you're barking up the wrong tree,' he remarked dubiously. 'Horrel appears to be everything a model citizen should be.'

'Granted,' Slade replied, 'but just the same I'd like a look at those papers. You can arrange it?'

'Yes, I'll see Judge Arbaugh right away,' the sheriff said. 'I'm sure I can talk him into letting you examine them, once he knows who and what you are. It isn't late. Let's go see the judge now.'

They repaired to the courthouse and found the judge in his office. Sheriff Wilson made his request; the jurist glanced inquiringly at Slade, his brows knitted.

'It's okay, Phil,' the sheriff assured him. 'Slade is one of Jim McNelty's men.'

'Then I guess it will be all right,' the judge agreed, regarding Slade with quickened interest. 'Anyhow, this young fellow has done so much good since he coiled his twine here, I'd be inclined to place confidence in him under any circumstances. I'll get the papers.'

He did so and Slade settled himself to examine the old papers while Sheriff Wilson and the judge smoked and talked.

For more than an hour Slade pored over the documents. Most of them were written in Spanish, almost archaic Spanish, Slade noted, and appeared perfectly authentic. The deed to the Spanish adventurer, Sebastian Menendez, interested him greatly. He read and re-read it, and again. To all appearances it was authentic, as appeared to be the signature of

134

Manuel Telo, Craig Telo's grandfather.

But another document interested him still more. This was the deed to the land signed by Menendez and transferring the holding to one Joseph Whitmer, from whom Rance Horrel had a deed to the property. He fingered it, examined both sides of the paper, studied the printed lettering—lettering of another and older day. One thing he noted with interest; the lettering was very clear-cut, as if new type had been employed in the printing. Abruptly he turned to Judge Arbaugh and the sheriff, holding the paper in his hand.

'As I understand, Judge, the court fight centered around the validity of Manuel Telo's signature on the deed granting the land to Menendez, did it not?'

'That's right,' answered the judge, 'and there appears no doubt but that the signature is valid.'

'Possibly,' Slade agreed, 'whether or not it belongs on this document. However it is really of little moment.'

'What do you mean?' asked the judge.

'I mean,' Slade said, 'that it is really of little importance unless heirs of Menendez should appear and file a claim to the land. As I gather, none ever have, and doubtless never will. The real crux of the whole controversy is here.' He tapped the paper in his hand as he spoke. 'This is the deed purported to have been signed by Sebastian Menendez and transferring the land to Joseph Whitmer, from whom Rance Horrel claims he bought the land.'

'He has a deed to show he did,' protested the judge.

'Naturally,' Slade smiled, 'a deed I understand was not questioned, the authenticity of which was conceded by both sides after little more than a superficial investigation. Practically impossible to prove it otherwise and with attention centered on the original grant to Menendez not given a great deal of attention. But if the deed apparently signed by Menendez is authentic, Craig Telo's claim to the land is voided.'

'Nothing was brought forward during the investigation to question the authenticity of that deed,' the judge declared belligerently.

'So I understand,' Slade smiled, one sensitive fingertip tracing the lettering on the paper. 'Judge, I'd like to borrow this paper for a few days.'

The judge loked a bit dubious. 'These are impounded papers, and I am responsible for them,' he said. 'Oh, all right, but for heaven's sake be careful of it. If anything happens to it, I'll find myself in a most embarrassing position when called upon to produce the papers. What I'm doing is most unethical and I wouldn't do it for anybody but a Texas Ranger. In fact, I wouldn't do it for just any Ranger, but one who enjoys Jim McNelty's confidence must be trustworthy.'

'Thank you,' Slade said. 'Now I'd like to have a sheet of clean white paper and some paper clips.'

While the others watched him with interest, he tore the sheet in half and clipped the halves over the deed in such a manner that only three printed lines were visible. He slipped the document in his pocket.

'And now what?' asked the sheriff.

'A little ride over to Alpen,' Slade replied. 'That newspaper editor at Alpen who espoused Craig Telo's cause, what's his name?'

'Lane Merriwell,' the sheriff replied.

'That man Merriwell is a demagogue and mad as a loon,' the judge declared angrily. 'I had to threaten him with a contempt citation to shut him up.'

' "Out of the mouths of babes and fools cometh wisdom," ' Slade quoted smilingly.

CHAPTER SIXTEEN

The ride to Alpen was not a particularly long or hard one. Slade started early and made good time. Upon reaching the town in the shadow of the Puertacitas Mountains, he at once looked up the editor, Lane Merriwell, who proved to be a pleasant, keen-eyed gentleman of middle age. Slade introduced himself and proceeded to state his business. He placed the old document, with only the three lines of printing—visible between the clipped sheets of paper, before the editor.

'What I wish to know, sir,' he explained, 'is whether you can identify the type used to print those lines.'

Merriwell peered at the lines, studied them through a magnifying glass.

'Why, yes.' he answered. 'They were printed from a fairly new pattern, one that simulates a much older pattern. It is frequently used in the final make-up of a story or article into which is inserted a letter or newspaper clipping supposedly of a much earlier date.'

'You are sure of that?' Slade asked.

'I'm sure,' the editor stated positively. 'However, I'll show you some corroborative evidence.'

He took down a huge tome from a shelf and turned the pages. 'Here we are,' he announced, 'a facsimile of the type in question. You can see for yourself that the two are identical.'

'It certainly looks that way, even to a layman's eyes,' Slade admitted. 'And when was this type first put into use?'

'Something under ten years back,' the editor replied. 'Let's see now. Yes, here is the date, a little more than nine years ago.'

'The three lines I showed you are supposed to have been printed many years before that,'

Slade said.

'Well, they weren't,' the editor declared. 'They were printed less than ten years ago.'

'And you are positive about the type—that it was not in use, say, twenty-five years ago.'

'You may take it, young man, that I am versed in the elements of my business,' the editor replied. 'I was a printer for many years and there is very little concerning type with which I am not familiar.'

Slade nodded. 'And you would be ready to go to court and swear the lines I showed you were printed on that paper less than ten years back?'

'I would,' said Merriwell. 'What is more, my testimony could be amply bolstered by the manufacturers of the product.'

'I see,' Slade said. He unclipped the covering sheets and handed the alleged deed to Merriwell.

The editor read the document and his eyes flashed. 'So!' he exclaimed. 'I was right all the time. I knew the hellion was crooked—as a snake in a cactus patch. We'll shove that scoundrel in jail!'

'No, we won't,' Slade said.

'Why?' demanded the editor.

'Because,' Slade stated grimly, 'I hope to eventually shove his neck into a hangman's noose. This land fraud business is a very minor matter when set against robbery and murder, of both which I am convinced Rance Horrel is

139

guilty. If we throw him in jail, I'll never be able to pin the more serious crimes on him. And even if he did go to prison for the land fraud, something never certain where a controversial matter such as this is concerned, in a few years he'd be out and all ready to set up in business again.'

'I guess that's right,' Merriwell admitted. 'But how does what you've learned help you?'

'It convinces me in my own mind that Horrel is off-color,' Slade explained. 'Now I can concentrate on him.'

'Guess that makes sense, too,' Merriwell nodded. 'What caused you to suspect Horrel?'

Slade replied with the single word he had spoken to Sheriff Wilson the night before, 'Greed.'

'Greed?'

'Yes. Where Horrel slipped, as the owlhoot brand usually does, in one way or another, was in evicting the little ranchers and *peon* farmers from the land they had occupied for generations, a very small part of the holding and land he didn't really need; that was an act of pure piggishness. If he had not done so, Craig Telo would not have flown into a rage and fought the case bitterly like he did. And in consequence, I would never have learned of old Manuel admonishing his son, Craig's father, to never dispossess the tenants and to always safeguard their welfare; which he certainly would not have done had he already

140

deeded the land to somebody else. That set me to thinking, and when I went over the old papers I quickly decided that the point on which the case could stand or fall was the deed supposedly made to Joseph Whitmer by Menendez, the Spanish adventurer. Examining it closely, I was struck by the exceedingly clear-cut and sharp indentations, which could only have been made by brand-new type. Didn't mean much, of course, but it did get me to thinking about the type. So I decided to do a little investigating. Appears it paid off.'

'It certainly did,' Merriwell agreed heartily. 'Wonder why Telo's lawyers didn't think of that angle?'

'I don't think the problem is a very obscure one,' Slade replied. 'When men, even smart men, become obsessed with an idea, they concentrate on it to the exclusion of all else. In this instance, the lawyers concentrated on trying to prove that the signature of Manuel Telo was a forgery, and were unsuccessful.'

Merriwell nodded. 'Sounds reasonable. If I can be of any further assistance to you, don't hesitate to call on me.'

'I won't,' Slade promised. 'Anyhow, if things don't work out right, we can very likely convict Horrel on the land fraud charge and put him out of circulation for a time, at least. Thanks for everything, sir, and I'll be seeing you.'

*   *   *

141

Slade rode back to Marta pleased with what he had accomplished but far from satisfied with things in general. He had definitely established that Rance Horrel had perpetrated a land fraud, and that was all. Such transactions were not uncommon to the Southwest, where land speculators of easy conscience were always digging into old files and records, especially those dealing with the Spanish grants, and coming up with schemes, some of them successful, of dubious legality and certainly unethical. The Horrel case was just an unusually daring and flagrant example. He just as definitely had *not* established that Rance Horrel was the pseudo Muerte Blanca or in any way responsible for the depredations that had been plaguing the section. Slade felt uneasy when he wondered if, by concentrating on Horrel, he was allowing the real culprit to operate without interference.

But if not Horrel, who? Well, he had asked the same question about Craig Telo, with negative results. But one thing was glaringly apparent: Rance Horrel was not averse to grabbing a crooked dollar. And his eviction of the tenants from the Telo land showed a callous disregard for human welfare. This made him an interesting possibility, at least.

It was well past dark when Slade reached Marta. He found the town buzzing.

'Three hellions robbed the Livermore bank,'

Pete Henry, the stable keeper, informed him. 'Shot the cashier bad and grabbed better'n twenty thousand dollars. Muerte Blanca, all right, white mask and everything. The nerve of the sidewinder! Pulled the robbery at the noon hour when there wasn't anybody in the bank but the cashier. Made a clean getaway into the hills. Some fellers tried to follow them but didn't have any luck. Sheriff Wilson rode down there, but I reckon he won't have any luck either. Those hellions know every crack and hole in the hills. Pity you weren't here. You might have lent him a hand.'

After seeing that all Shadow's wants were provided for, Slade made his way to the Montezuma and something to eat. When he entered he saw Craig Telo with his left shoulder bandaged and his left arm in a sling, but apparently in excellent spirits. He was the center of a group of cattlemen with whom he appeared to be on very friendly terms. Spotting Slade, he disengaged himself from the group and joined him at the bar.

'Well,' he said, 'I got to feeling you didn't approve of what I was doing, so I went to work and told everybody where I got that money and how and all the details. I don't think it did me any harm.'

'It didn't,' Slade assured him. 'You may have been aggravating some busybodies, as you call them, but you were also making a lot of decent people wonder about you, which

143

wasn't good. The time may come when you'll need friends who trust you and believe in you—and no man can say for sure that such a time won't ever come to him—and you could have found yourself in a lonely and unpleasant position.'

'I've a notion you're right,' Telo said soberly. 'In fact, I guess you're always right.'

'Not always, I'm afraid,' Slade smiled.

'I suppose you heard about the bank robbery?' Telo remarked.

'Yes, Pete Henry told me,' Slade replied.

'I was here when the word came,' Telo added. 'Funny, Sheriff Wilson came over and spoke to me for the first time in quite a while. Said it was a pity I wasn't in better shape or he'd ask me to go along. Said he figured I deserved a crack at the hellions if there was a chance to get one. He's convinced those two devils who tried to rob me belonged to the Muerte Blanca outfit.'

'He's quite probably right,' Slade answered. 'Well, I'm going to have something to eat— feel gaunt as a gutted snowbird. Join me?'

'I've already eaten,' Telo said. 'I'll go back and gab with the boys some more. Feels good to have folks come up and talk to me again; they haven't been doing that much of late. Be seeing you!'

He ambled off. Slade sat down at a nearby table and ordered everything in sight.

CHAPTER SEVENTEEN

Slade visited Sheriff Wilson the following morning and found him in a very bad temper.

'No luck, eh?' he remarked.

'None at all,' growled the sheriff. 'They had many hours start and it was a cold trail. About the only thing I could ascertain is that they were curving around in this general direction. Perhaps I should have ridden to the Smuggler on the chance of intercepting them.'

'I doubt if they would have used that route again after what happened to them after the stage robbery,' Slade said. 'Nobody got a good look at them, of course?'

'They were masked,' the sheriff answered. 'The tall one wearing a white rag over his face in the accepted Muerte Blanca style. They're still playing that angle to a fare-you-well. Some of the townsfolk tried to follow them, but a little lead whistling about their ears and a nicked hand for one sort of discouraged them and they gave up the chase.'

'Good thing they did, I expect,' Slade said. 'Otherwise they would very likely have bulged into an ambush and got blown from under their hats.'

'What did you learn over at Alpen?' the sheriff asked.

Slade told him. The sheriff swore in

incredulous amazement.

'So Horrel did pull a whizzer!' he exclaimed. 'That ornery horned toad! Going to drop a loop on him?'

Slade shook his head. 'The land fraud is a comparatively small matter,' he explained. 'I hope to corral him for something much more serious.'

'You figure then he's the gent who wears a white rag over his face?'

'That's my opinion, but I may have a devil of a time proving it, unless I have the luck to catch him redhanded in something,' Slade replied. 'Here's the Menendez-Whitmer deed. You can give it back to the judge. I've a notion he'll feel more comfortable with it in his hands.'

'What shall I tell him?' asked the sheriff.

'Nothing,' Slade said. 'I don't think he'd talk, but his sense of justice and his natural anger at being hoodwinked like he was might cause him to move against Horrel. Just thank him for me and tell him I'll have a talk with him later.'

Wilson stowed away the paper, shaking his head in admiration. 'Son, you're smart, all right,' he declared. 'No wonder old Jim thinks so highly of you.'

'He won't think so highly if I don't start doing better than I have of late,' Slade said.

'Anyhow, you've been thinning out the hellions,' the sheriff said.

146

'Yes,' Slade admitted, 'but I'll repeat what I said before, the head is still running around loose and that sort of a head grows another body fast. He appeared to be thoroughly familiar with the section when he showed up here the first time, a couple of years back. I've a notion he'd been studying conditions here, had dug up all he could about the Telo land grants, and saw a chance to grab onto a nice holding and at the same tine provide an excellent cover-up for his other activities. A smart hombre, all right, and one with plenty of guts and no conscience. That is, if I'm not barking up the wrong tree, as you mentioned before.'

'I've a feeling you aren't,' said the sheriff. 'And I reckon him coming in and complaining about stolen cows is part of the blind.'

'Quite likely,' Slade agreed, 'although there always has been, and I suppose always will be, considerable cattle pilfering in this section. He may really be losing a few critters now and then. His holding is to the south and in a good location, from wideloopers' viewpoint, for the running off of cows.'

'Guess so,' admitted the sheriff. 'Reckon he'll be showing up soon again with a list of what he's lost and detailing all the spots and stripes on the critters.'

Slade was struck by a sudden thought. 'That last list he brought in, have you still got it?' he asked.

'Sure, right here in the drawer,' said the sheriff.

'He rummaged about and produced the list in question. Slade drew forth a crumpled slip which he placed beside the list the wage voucher he had taken from the pocket of the dead smuggler killer.

'Take a look,' he said.

Sheriff Wilson peered at the two slips of paper, his brows knitting.

'Well, what do you say?' Slade asked.

'I'd say both were written by the same man,' the sheriff announced. 'Where'd you get this thing?'

Slade told him. The sheriff swore explosively. 'That settles it,' he declared. 'We've got the sidewinder tied up. Shall I drop a loop on him?'

'On what charge?'

'Reckon murder would do as well as any,' said the sheriff.

'And the proof? All you have is evidence that a scalawag once worked for Rance Horrel. Just as we have evidence that a couple of them once worked for Craig Telo. You can't jail a man for making a mistake in his hiring. He'd laugh at you, and be justified in doing so. The importance of what we've just learned is that it's another link, undependable though it is, indicating that Horrel associated with a questionable character, but no help in proving that he knowingly associated with one. It's of value, in that it bolsters my personal opinion of Horrel and makes me less fearful of doing an innocent man an injustice and at the same time giving the really guilty hellion free rein. See?'

'Yes, I see,' grumbled the sheriff, 'but it still looks like we're getting nowhere fast.'

'Maybe we'll get a break,' Slade hoped cheerfully. 'More likely, I'd say, he'll slip somewhere, as his sort always does, sooner or later. I'm banking heavily on that.'

'I hope you're right,' sighed Wilson. 'Things sure aren't breaking well of late, and folks are saying things about me that don't make nice listening. I've a notion Jim McNelty is getting some more letters.'

'Wouldn't be surprised,' Slade admitted 'Was the bank cashier seriously wounded?'

'He'll pull through,' replied the sheriff. 'Doctor got to him in a hurry, otherwise he'd have very likely bled to death. Those devils sure had cold nerve and must have studied the bank thoroughly before they pulled the job. They evidently learned that the cashier was usually alone right after twelve noon. An alley runs in back of the bank and it's lined with warehouses with blank walls facing the alley, which starts over close to the edge of town and the brush. They came to the bank by way of that alley, smashed open the back door with one rush and were inside before Grumley, the cashier, knew what was happening. He made the mistake of grabbing for a gun and the tall hellion let him have it. Slug went through the upper chest and knocked him unconscious. Reckon they figured it killed him. Anyhow, they didn't bother him any more. Cleaned the vault and were out the back door and gone before folks who heard the shot figured what was going on. A couple of fellers saw them cut into the brush and grabbed horses from the racks and set out after them and, as I told you, gave up when lead began coming a mite too close for comfort. Regular Muerte Blanca chore, all right. That is, the Muerte Blanca we got operating in the section now. The original never pulled anything like that that I ever heard of.'

'He was a fuzzy little kitten compared with the sidewinder we have to deal with,' Slade agreed. He sat silent for some moments, then spoke. 'One angle is beginning to bother me,' he said.

'What's that?' asked the sheriff.

'I'm wondering,' Slade said, 'if the hellion is planning to pull out. He appears to be intent on grabbing off as much money as possible in the shortest possible time, regardless of risk. The raid on the Livermore bank smacked of the reckless daring of a desperate man. I believe there are only a couple of his men left alive, three at the most, and one more big job and they'd be well-heeled and all ready to slide out for Mexico or someplace and after lying

150

low a while set up in business elsewhere.'

'He has seven or eight hands working for him on the spread,' Wilson pointed out.

'Yes, and I'm ready to wager they haven't the slightest inkling of what's going on,' Slade answered. 'He'd hire honest cowboys to tend his cattle, keep his owlhoot bunch under cover somewhere. He's too shrewd to use his ranch hands in his outlaw activities or to use his raiders on the ranch. That way, one little slip and his game would be exposed. Counting up the men he's recently lost, I feel pretty sure he has no more than two or three of his sidewinders left.'

'But what makes you think he may plan to pull out?' the sheriff asked.

'As I said, the latest raid he pulled hints that he's getting jittery,' Slade explained. 'He may have recognized me as a Ranger and figures the Rangers are closing in on him. I may have worn a tail when I rode to Alpen yesterday, with the fellow staying far behind out of sight and only closing in on me when I reached town. If so, quite likely I was spotted visiting Merriwell, the editor of the Clarion, the man who insisted from the first that the land grab was a fraud. Why would I be visiting him? Because I must have dug up something. Horrel would figure that very likely the jig was up so far as the land deal was concerned and he'd have to leave in all events before that was pinned on him. I think he's just smart enough,

151

however, to realize that I, as a Ranger, would be reluctant to grab him on such a minor charge and decide I won't make a move until I have something really serious on him. All conjecture, of course, but if I was in his place I think that's the conclusion at which I would arrive. Anyhow, I'm gambling on it and hope to forestall him or drop a loop on him when he attempts his next raid.'

'But how the devil are you going to do it?' the sheriff asked wearily.

'I don't know,' Slade admitted frankly. 'But one thing I'm going to do, I'm going to put my Mexican boy to work. He was the only survivor when Miguel Allende and his smugglers were murdered. The only thing he thinks about is revenging his murdered brothers and he'll jump at a chance to even the score. I'm sure he's trustworthy and he's intelligent. He's enough of an *Indio* to be able to move silently as a snake and keep under cover. It would be impossible for me to ride in and out of town without sooner or later being spotted. Nobody knows about him and nobody will pay him any mind, even if he is seen.

With his help we should be able to keep tabs on the gent day and night. I'm convinced he has a hole-up not too far away, aside from his ranch house. If I can locate that hole-up, that will be the first and most important step toward dropping a loop on him. I'm going to look up Pedro right now. Be seeing you a little

152

later.'

Slade found the Mexican youth at the little *cantina* at the edge of town; there were no patrons in the place at the moment. The proprietor, a plump and jolly Mexican, greeted Slade with the greatest respect. He brought wine that exuded a bouquet like to the fragrance of crushed roses, smiled and nodded and left Slade and Pedro alone at a table.

'Got a chore for you, *muchacho*,' Slade said. 'Handle it right and you may get a chance to even things up a bit.'

Pedro's eyes flashed; he leaned forward eagerly. 'I am ready, *Capitan*,' he answered. 'Anything! I am ready!'

Slade rolled a cigarette before speaking, then he proceeded to explain.

'You recall the first ranch house we passed on the way to town? The RH.'

'The *casa* of the *Señor* Horrel,' Pedro replied. 'Yes, I remember.'

'To the west, beyond the trail, there are low brush-covered hills, you will recall. I think you wouldn't have any trouble holing up in those hills and keeping under cover. From their east slopes you should be able to see anything that goes on around the RH ranch house, even at night, with the starlight bright as it is, and a moon part of the night. It'll be a night chore, for I don't think anything will happen in the daytime. Watch and see if any strange men visit the ranch house. And if you see the *Señor*

153

Horrel riding off alone at night do you think you could trail him?'

'*Capitan*,' Pedro answered, 'I am from the Sinaloa mountains and I have *Indio* blood. My mother was the daughter of a Yaqui chief and I lived much with the Yaquis. I can move and remain unseen even as does *El Culebra* when he slithers through the chaparral in search of a packrat to stay his hunger. *Si*, I can trail him, and he will not know it.'

'Good!' Slade said. 'Well, you've got your powders. Slip out of town tonight; and pack provisions along with you so you can hole up for a few days without coming back to town unless you have some word for me. And I'll be seeing you out there, too, most any time.'

'And when I hear you coming, *Capitan*, I will be most careful not to shoot,' the Mexican boy promised. Slade smiled slightly but did not comment. He sat silent, for he knew by the youth's expression that he had something to say and was turning the advisability over in his mind. There is no rushing an *Indio* when he is debating something with himself, so Slade gave him time to think it out. Finally Pedro spoke.

'*Capitan*,' he said, 'I have heard a strange story—a story that says Muerte Blanca the accurst is dead.'

'Yes, he is dead,' Slade said quietly. 'He has been dead a year.'

The boy's eyes widened. 'But, *Capitan*,' he

protested, 'the tall man with the mask of white, with my own eyes I saw him.'

'Muerte Blanca is dead,' Slade repeated, 'but, Pedro, a wise man once wrote, "The evil that men do lives after them."' And the evil spawned by Muerte Blanca is still very much alive.'

'And another has taken his place?'

'That's right. Or, rather, another is trading on Muerte Blanca's reputation to frighten and confuse people and cause them to search futilely for a non-existent person while he, who is very real indeed, works further evil.'

'And he is—' Pedro began, his eyes flashing.

'As yet I have no proof who he is,' Slade interrupted. 'Remember that, Pedro, and don't go jumping at conclusions. It is very easy to make a mistake. For some time I was making one, and I don't care to repeat the performance. When I know for sure who was responsible for the murder of your brothers I will tell you. Until then your chore is to watch, and report to me anything you may see or learn. If violence is offered you by anyone, defend yourself, but don't start anything. Understand?'

'I understand, and I will do as you say,' Pedro promised. Slade felt sure he would be good as his word.

'Want me to speak to your boss and arrange for you to be away from the job a few days?' he suggested.

'It is not necessary,' Pedro replied, 'I will tell him that El Halcon commands, and when El Halcon commands, one obeys.'

'Okay, we'll let it go at that,' Slade chuckled. 'Be seeing you.'

Slade returned to the sheriff's office. Wilson glanced at him expectantly.

'All set,' Slade replied in answer to the sheriff's look. 'I've a notion the scheme will pay off. Pedro's a smart boy.'

'He'd better be or he'll very likely end up buzzard bait,' the sheriff grunted. 'He's going up against a sidewinder for fair.'

'I'm confident he can take care of himself, otherwise I wouldn't have let him take the chance,' Slade replied. 'I think he'll do exactly as I told him and not push forward into trouble. Under those circumstances I hardly see how he can come to harm. And I figure to keep an eye on him, although he won't know it.'

CHAPTER EIGHTEEN

Several uneventful days passed. And then, well after midnight, when Slade was sitting in the Montezuma talking with Craig Telo, Pedro entered, sauntered to the bar and ordered a drink. Over the rim of his glass he casually glanced about the room, caught Slade's eye and inclined his head the merest fraction. Slade's slight answering nod was barely perceptible as he went on conversing with Telo.

Pedro took his time over his drink, finally finished it and left the saloon as casually as he had entered it, attracting not the slightest notice. Slade talked on with Telo for a little longer, then said good night to the rancher and also left. Outside he loitered along the street, apparently oblivious of his surroundings, but in reality keeping a close watch on all that went on and never losing sight of the Montezuma's swinging doors. Confident at last that he was neither being watched nor followed, he quickened his step and a little later turned in at the *cantina* near the edge of town.

There were a number of Mexicans in the place, some of whom nodded in friendly fashion. Slade found a vacant table and sat down. Pedro appeared from behind the partition that shut off the kitchen and courteously requested his order, handing Slade a printed wine list.

As Slade appeared to study the list, Pedro spoke, his voice barely audible, his lips moving not at all.

'For three nights, *Capitan*, nothing happened,' he said. 'But tonight, well past dark, the *Señor* Horrel rode forth and turned south. I followed as you directed, keeping in the shadow of the growth. He rode the

Smuggler Trail for several miles then turned off to the west, following what looked to be but a game track. He passed very close to where I was hidden, ready to grasp my horse's nose did it attempt to neigh. After he had passed, again I followed. I followed for several more miles, through shallow canyons and along the slopes of ridges. Finally, in a narrow gorge and almost hidden from view, there appeared an old cabin in which a light burned. The *Señor* Horrel rode to the cabin, dismounted and entered. I waited for some time, growing very curious as to what was within that cabin. Finally my curiosity was so great that I dismounted and slipped through the brush until I was close to the cabin window, which stood open.'

Pedro paused. Slade gestured to the wine list and Pedro bent over the table as if in answer to a question. He spoke again.

'Within the cabin, which appeared to have but one room, sat the *Señor* Horrel and two more men, evil-looking men. There were bunks built against the wall, cooking utensils beside an old stove, some chairs and a table. There were many *escopetas*—rifles—standing in racks against a wall. The *Señor* Horrel and the two men sat at the table on which was a bottle and glasses. They were speaking.'

'Did you hear what was said?' Slade asked, gesturing to the wine list, over which Pedro bent attentively.

'*Capitan*, my inspiration came too late and I heard but little,' Pedro admitted regretfully. 'I but heard the *Señor* Horrel say, "So that's how it'll be done. Ben, you will be there with the horses, and no slips. I'm depending on you and there won't be any time to spare. Okay, you've got your powders. Mind you, no slips." He stood up and I knew he would leave the cabin soon, so I hurried back to my horse. He rode away and I followed. Straight back to his RH *casa* he rode. I circled the ranch house and rode to town.'

'Sounds darn interesting,' Slade said. 'A pity you didn't hear more, but maybe we can learn something from that cabin. Hole up directly opposite the ranch house tomorrow night and I will join you some time after dark. You can find your way back to the cabin in the gorge?'

'Of a certainty, *Capitan*. If I once ride a trail I do not forget.'

With a nod he darted for the kitchen, ostensibly to fetch Slade's order. He returned soon afterward, with a wine bottle, a glass and a smoking dish containing something that gave forth a most appetizing smell.

Slade consumed Pedro's offering in a leisurely fashion and drank of the excellent wine, the meanwhile thinking deeply. It appeared there was definitely something in the wind. Horrel was undoubtedly up to some devilment, something that required horses being at some particular spot. Slade wracked

159

his brains for an answer to the conundrum and found none. A devil of a pity Pedro hadn't heard more; but he didn't, and Slade felt he had done remarkably well as it was. Perhaps the cabin would provide some clue to what Horrel was planning, or perhaps Pedro might be able to spot something else. Slade hoped so. A little later, he went to bed.

* * *

Not knowing when he would get more rest, things shaping up as they were, Slade slept late. He had a leisurely breakfast, loafed around the town a bit, had a talk with Sheriff Wilson and after eating his dinner retired to his room. Shortly after dark he slipped out of town and gained the Smuggler Trail which he followed until he had passed Craig Telo's Bar O ranch house. Then he turned off and for some miles rode in the shadow of the brush covered hills to the west, finally sending Shadow up the slope for another quarter of a mile; now he was almost opposite the site of Horrel's RH *casa*.

In a little clearing where grass grew and a trickle of water seeped from under a cliff he left Shadow; the rest of the jaunt would be on foot.

* * *

160

Pedro, the Mexican youth, lay on his stomach under an arch of chaparral. From this point of vantage he could clearly see the shadowy mass of the RH ranch house with its drive winding down to the Smuggler Trail. Nothing escaped his watchful eyes. He saw the lights in the bunk house wink out until all was darkness and knew the tired cowhands had settled down to rest. No light showed in the ranch house itself, but none had shown the night Rance Horrel rode to the rendezvous at the lonely cabin in the gorge miles to the south and west. Pedro was taking no chances on missing a bet. He was wondering whether he could risk lighting a shuck cigarette when a voice spoke at his elbow.

'Anything new, *muchacho*?'

Pedro flopped straight up from the ground a foot. He came down squirming around and clutching his rifle, his breath exhaling in a frightened whoosh!

'Take it easy,' Slade chuckled. 'Did I give you a start?'

'*Capitan!*' Pedro gasped. 'How in the name of *El Dios* did you do it?'

'Do what?' Slade asked innocently as he squatted on his heels and began rolling a cigarette.

'Creep up on me as you did. Not even a Yaqui brave could do so without me hearing. My ears are as the ears of *el lobo*—the wolf— but I heard you not.'

161

'Well, I never hung out with the Yaquis, but I did spend quite a bit of time, when I was much younger, with a little tribe of Karankawas, about the only Karanks left in Texas, and I don't think they have any equal at brush tracking. They taught me considerable.'

'If the good fathers of the Mission taught me not wrong and I understand properly that word, it is much too weak,' Pedro declared with conviction. 'Surely, *Capitan*, you move as does the little shadow that runs across the grassland and loses itself at sunset.'

Slade chuckled again. 'Here, have a cigarette,' he said, passing the brain tablet to his companion and beginning another for himself, 'I think it will do your nerves good. I suppose I shouldn't have startled you that way, but I recollect you mentloning in the *cantina* that when I visited you, you would hear me and be careful not to shoot. Just wanted to make sure you didn't make a mistake.'

Pedro's grimace showed plain in the light of the match he cupped carefully in his hands to touch to the cigarette.

'You make the joke of me, *Capitan*,' he protested.

Slade laughed and puffed on his cigarette. 'You're doing all right,' he said.

They finished the cigarettes and Slade stood up. 'Now let's go have a look at that cabin,' he suggested. 'That is if you can find it again in the dark.'

'I can find it,' Pedro declared confidently.

Slade secured Shadow and Pedro his mount from where it was tethered back in the brush. They rode south in the shadow of the hills.

For a number of miles they rode, hearing nothing but the occasional call of a night bird or the lonely, beautiful plaint of a hunting wolf and seeing nothing but the glittering stars overhead and the black blocks of thickets scattered over the rangeland. After a while Pedro turned due west into a canyon which emptied into still another. He turned south again and a little later entered the mouth of a narrow gorge with rocky sides. Here the gloom was thick and nothing broke the silence save the purling of a little stream over its pebbly bed. Five minutes more and Pedro slowed his mount to a walk, then pulled him to a halt.

'It is there, *Capitan*,' he whispered.

Peering through the darkness, Slade could just make out the solid bulk of the weatherbeaten building. No light shone and nothing blunted the sharp edge of the stillness.

For long minutes Slade sat studying the cabin. 'Looks like there's nobody at home,' he finally whispered. 'Okay, you stop here with the horses—Shadow will stay put but I'm not so sure about your critter and we don't want to get stranded. I'm going to have a look-see. Pretty sure there's nobody around but it's best not to take chances.'

He slipped from the saddle and glided

forward, taking advantage of all the cover that was offered. Without mishap he reached the closed door of the building. Here he paused, peering and listening. Nowhere could he discern movement and the silence remained intense. He reached out and gave the door a gentle push. It responded easily to his touch and he slipped through the opening.

The door swung wide open with a sudden screech of unoiled hinges. Across the room sounded a rustling creak. Slade hurled himself sideways away from the door. A gun blazed in the darkness and the bullet thudded into the wall inches from his head. Another flash and he gasped as a second slug ripped a stinging furrow along his ribs and nearly knocked him off his feet. Then his own guns let go with a rattling crash.

Back and forth through the murk gushed the orange flashes. The cabin rocked to the thunder of the reports. Slade felt the wind of passing lead. A slug ripped his sleeve. Another tore through the crown of his hat. Then he abruptly realized that no more missiles were coming toward him. He crouched low, his thumbs hooked over the cocked hammers of his Colts. From the darkness across the room came a gurgling sound, a choking cough, a whistling gasp followed by silence through which the patter of Pedro's feet across the clearing sounded loud.

'Hold it!' Slade called and instantly shifted

position. The sound of footsteps ceased, and across the room was nothing but stillness. Slade called out again as he glided along the wall, 'I think everything's under control. Strike a match and we'll make sure.'

While Pedro was fumbling for the match, Slade was beset by all sorts of unpleasant apprehensions. Pedro might have made a mistake and this was the wrong cabin. If so, he might have shot some innocent prospector or trapper who naturally opened fire when his door swung open. He breathed a sigh of relief as the match flickered and the tiny flame reflected back from the glistening barrels of a row of rifles leaning against a wall, just as the Mexican boy had described them.

The match also revealed a lamp standing on a table near the center of the room. Slade holstered his guns, struck another match and touched it to the wick. The sudden glow showed a man sprawled on the floor with the disordered blankets of the bunk in which he had been sleeping lying beside him. Slade strode forward ready for instant action, but a glance told him the man was dead.

'Got him through the neck,' he told Pedro after a brief examination. 'He came darn close to getting me, though. I lost some skin from my ribs. A couple of inches farther to the left and I wouldn't be telling you about it.'

Pedro peered into the dead face. 'This is not the man Ben to whom the *Señor* Horrel spoke,' he announced. 'This is the other hombre.'

'And Ben was the one Horrel told to be somewhere with horses,' Slade remarked musingly. 'Where and for what purpose I sure wish I knew.'

'More than two men have lived here,' said Pedro. 'Look—the shelves are loaded with food and there are more bunks and many blankets. And many rifles,' he added glancing at the row against the wall.

'Yes, it was the hangout for the bunch, all right,' Slade said. 'Not so many of them as there was in the beginning,' he added grimly. 'Here's a pot of coffee on the stove, still warm.'

He procured a couple of tin cups from a shelf—and filled them with the steaming liquid.

'This won't go bad,' he said, passing a cup to Pedro. 'Then we'll look this shack over and dispose of that carcass. Should be a horse somewhere around. We don't want the body found here when somebody shows up, as I figure they will sooner or later.'

A search of the cabin discovered nothing of significance save further evidence that it had been occupied at one time or another by a number of men. The dead man was an ornery-looking specimen with no outstanding features. His pockets revealed only regulation odds and ends and a goodly sum of money which Slade handed to Pedro.

'Go see if you can find this jigger's horse,' Slade told him. 'Must be one around somewhere.'

Very quickly, Pedro located a leanto behind the cabin, under which a single horse was tethered, although there was riding gear for more than one animal. Following Slade's directions, he got a rig on the cayuse. Then they carried the body out and lashed it to the saddle.

'Do we take him to town?' Pedro asked.

'No, that would advertise our presence here,' Slade replied. 'I have a little plan building up in the back of my mind and its success depends on the rest of the bunch, if they come back, and I think they will, not learning of anybody being here. We'll pack him into the chaparral, a ways and cover him over with brush. The horse can fend for himself after we remove the rig. Sooner or later somebody will pick him up.'

Before leaving the cabin, Slade carefully wiped up the blood that had flowed from the outlaw's death wound. There were so many grease spots scattered around that he felt sure the stain would not be noticed. Making sure there were no signs of their visit left, he blew out the lamp and they secured their horses and set out on the return journey to town. Several miles beyond the first canyon that the trail to the cabin entered, they dumped the body, and

167

the rig taken from the horse, into a crevice and covered it with brush.

'Now when the others show up at the cabin and don't find that hellion, they'll likely figure he went off to get drunk or something,' Slade said. 'Anyhow, let's hope so.'

'Shall I remain on watch?' Pedro asked as they rode north.

'No,' Slade decided. 'You'll ride on to town and hole up in the *cantina* till I figure what's in the works. I've a hunch something will happen in the next day or so to govern our next move.'

Dawn was firing the sky with saffron and tremulous pink as they drew near Marta. Slade rode on ahead, leaving Pedro to follow. He stabled Shadow, made sure all his wants were provided for and then headed for bed, fairly satisfied with the results of the night's work.

But it was more bull luck than anything else, he told himself. I should have known better than to go bulging into that cabin like I did. Should have figured that one of the hellions might be sleeping there. Well, reckon you can't think of everything.

*　　　*　　　*

Slade arose late in the afternoon. After eating his breakfast at the little restaurant across the street, he dropped in at the sheriff's office.

Sheriff Wilson was not present. Crane, his chief deputy was in charge.

'Bert rode over to the Fiddle-Back ranch

168

house,' he explained. 'Old Wirt McDowell who owns the spread is bedridden with sciatica. He and Bert are old *amigos* and he's been asking for Bert to come and gab with him a while. Doubt if Bert will be back tonight. It's a long ride.'

Leaving the office, Slade made his way to the little *cantina* where he found Pedro performing his usual duties.

'Stick around close,' he told the Mexican boy. 'I've got a hunch something may break most any time now.'

Something was due to break, and very soon, something that perturbed Slade not a little.

Well after dark, Slade entered the Montezuma and found Craig Telo there.

'Looks like our *amigo* Horrel is taking himself a little trip,' Telo observed. 'I saw him get on the westbound Sunrise Limited packing along a big carpetbag when she pulled out about ten minutes ago.'

'The devil you did!' Slade exclaimed.

'Uh-huh, and from the size of that bag, I reckon he figures to be away quite a while. Hope he never comes back!'

Slade abruptly found himself wondering if Horrel would ever come back. He might be pulling out for good. But somehow Slade didn't think so. He recalled Horrel's injunction to the man Ben, as reported by Pedro—'You will be there with the horses.'

Which meant, Slade was confident, that

169

Horrel had some enterprise planned and somewhere in the section. But why the devil did he board the westbound flyer? The answer would be provided, and soon.

CHAPTER NINETEEN

The Sunrise Limited was late and making up time. Siderods clanking, headlight glaring, the exhaust a purring chuckle, the great locomotive rushed through the night. The old engineer, bouncing about on his seatbox, peered out the window, one hand on the wide-open throttle, the other on the automatic brake valve lever. Both injectors were wide open, pouring streams of water into the straining boiler. The cab was abruptly filled with a red glare and the musical clang of a shovel as the 'tallowpot' hopped down from his seat, flung open the fire door and expertly scattered coal into the raging furnace. The lights of Marta were far behind, with Van Horn, Sierra Blanca and El Paso far ahead. The engineer glanced at the steam gauge hand quivering against the two-hundred pound pressure mark and eased the reverse bar up another notch; the speed of the locomotive increased a little. Clouds of black smoke streaked with steam rolled back over the long train as the fireman put in another fire. The whistle wailed, rousing a hundred flying echoes. The rumble of the wheels beat back from cliff and grove.

'We'll hit El Paso on time!' whooped the fireman. 'Shove her along, Tom, shove her along!'

In the express car next to the engine, the express messenger bent over his records. He did not hear the end door of the car, supposed to be locked, open and close. Nor did he see the tall man who slipped in silently, a white mask covering his features, in one hand a big carpetbag, in the other a long-barrelled gun.

Some premonition of evil or a slight sound caused the messenger to turn his head. Eyes dilating, he stared straight into the black gun muzzle. The man who held it spoke harshly, his voice muffled behind the folds of white cloth.

'Open that safe, and be quick about it,' he ordered, gesturing to the big strongbox that was bolted to the floor and the car wall.

The shivering messenger hesitated. Then his staring eyes saw that the hammer of the big gun was at full cock, the trigger drawn all the way back, with only the weight of the robber's thumb to keep it from falling on the firing pin. And as he stared, the thumb began to slip back toward the milled tip. He scrambled from his chair, knelt before the safe and began twirling the combination knob. The door swung open, revealing thick packets of bills and several

171

canvas sacks.

The bandit moved forward a step and thrust the big carpetbag at the messenger.

'Shove the stuff in that,' he ordered.

The trembling messenger obeyed. When the last packet was in the bag, he started to rise to his feet. A sideways slashing blow of the heavy gun barrel and he fell to the floor senseless, blood pouring from his gashed scalp. The robber snapped the catch of the bag, picked it up and moved to the rear door of the car. He listened a moment, opened the door and slipped through, closing it behind him. He locked it with a key that shouldn't have been in his possession. He did not enter the following coach but stood poised on the end sill of the express car, holding onto a grab-iron and peering into the darkness.

The whistle blew a long blast. The chuckling exhaust snapped off, the safety valve rose with a thunderous boom, the blower roared as the fireman twirled a valve, raising the smoke. The long train quickly lost speed.

Two hours later, Slade was still in the Montezuma conversing with Craig Telo when a wild-eyed man waving a sheet of yellow paper rushed in. Slade recognized him as the railroad telegraph operator.

'Where's the sheriff?' he bawled. 'Anybody know where I can find the sheriff?'

Slade seized him by the arm and stayed his progress. 'Sheriff is out of town,' he said.

'What's the matter?'

'Muerte Blanca robbed the Sunrise Limited express car,' the operator chattered. 'Got away with close to fifty thousand. Knocked the messenger cold. They didn't find out about it till they stopped at Sierra Blanca where express was to be loaded. Messenger came to and told 'em about it. He said it must have been Muerte Blanca—he wore a white mask, and—'

'Hold it,' Slade said. 'What is the first stop the Limited makes after leaving Marta?'

'Stops about twenty miles to the west where there's a pumping station, to take water,' the operator replied.

'And when did the robbery occur, according to the messenger?'

'Not long after they pulled out of Marta.'

'And before they reached the water tank?'

'That's the way I understood it,' admitted the messenger.

'Okay,' Slade said. 'Try and find Crane, the chief deputy, and tell him what you told me. He may be at the Root Hog or maybe the Three Deuces; he hangs out at those places.'

The operator rushed out. Slade turned to Telo. 'Be seeing you,' he said and left the saloon.

As he hurried to the little *cantina* on the edge of town, Slade estimated the distance Horrel would have to cover from where the water tank was located to the cabin in the gorge, for he was confident that Horrel left the train when it stopped for water. Ben would have horses waiting and, Slade felt sure, they would head for the cabin to pick up their other companion whom they very likely did not know was dead. Then, he believed, they would divide the loot and hightail for Mexico by way of little known trails. And if they got started for the Rio Grande, running them down would be a difficult task indeed.

Now Slade believed Horrel really intended to pull out. He'd gotten his stake and would try to leave the country.

'Got to drop a loop on him at the cabin or not at all,' be muttered. 'And it's going to be close. They won't hang out there for long. When they don't find the other jigger there they'll very likely figure something is wrong and not waste any time getting in the clear. It's going to be close.'

However, he felt he was honor bound to give Pedro a chance to be in on the kill. When he reached the *cantina*, he quickly located the Mexican boy.

'Get your horse,' he ordered tersely. 'We're riding for the showdown, I hope.'

Ten minutes later they thundered out of town in a cloud of dust. The time for concealment was past. Now it was a race against the inexorably moving hands of Slade's watch.

As he rode, Slade slipped the star of the

174

Rangers from its secret pocket in his broad leather belt and pinned it to his shirt front. Pedro's eyes bulged as he stared at the famous symbol of justice, law and order.

'So that is what you are, *Capitan!*' he marveled. 'Well, I should have guessed.'

'Yes, I'm a peace officer and must conduct myself as one,' Slade said.

Mile after mile rolled past under the speeding hoofs. Slade estimated the distance covered, the distance yet to go. Finally he shook his head.

'Time's running out,' he told the Mexican. 'I'm going to ride on ahead. Follow as fast as you can.'

'But *Capitan*, you take the chance,' Pedro protested. 'There will be two of them, perhaps more.'

'Have to risk it,' Slade replied. 'At the rate we're going, they'll very likely pull out before we get there. I've a notion they'll hustle when they don't find the other hellion waiting for them. Horrel is shrewd and will guess something went wrong. Be seeing you!'

Muttering prayers to his patron saint, Pedro urged his horse to greater speed, but the great black steadily pulled away from him and soon was lost in the gloom.

Slade rode at top speed but watchful and alert, for there was always the chance that Horrel and his companion might have been delayed by something or other. And should they hear him coming and hole up and wait, the results for him would very likely be disastrous.

However, he reached the mouth of the first canyon without anything untoward occurring. Here he was forced to slacken his speed, for the track was rough and hazardous. On he forged, past frowning cliffs and black fangs of chimney rock, between bristles of dark and twisted junipers, and firs, with clumps of chaparral rising silent and ominous on either hand, any of which could give shelter to a score of outlaws.

But the silence of the star-burned night remained unbroken. There was no sign of movement apparent when he reached the second canyon even narrower and more rugged than the first. The gloom was intense and he was forced to slow Shadow almost to a walk. After what seemed a very long time he reached the mouth of the gorge in which the cabin stood. Here he pulled up and for some minutes sat peering and listening. He had no desire to meet the outlaws coming through the narrow gut. Finally he rode on again at a slow walk. Abruptly he pulled to a halt. Through the thick gloom shone a faint glow of light.

Gradually he realized that it came from the dirty window of the cabin. Somebody in there, all right. He slipped to the ground and crept forward with the greatest caution, reaching without mishap a point where he could peer through the window.

The glass was so encrusted with grime that he could not make out details. All he could be sure of was that two forms sat at the table busy at something. If anybody else was in the cabin he was out of sight.

Slade did not believe the cabin sheltered others than Rance Horrel and the man Ben. If he was making a mistake, well, it would very likely be his last. He might be able to get the jump on the pair at the table, but if there was a third man in the room, the advantage would all be his. The murmur of voices came faintly through the window and Slade decided that only two persons were speaking. He resolved to take a chance. Gliding around the corner of the building, he paused in front of the closed door, loosened his guns in their sheaths, listened a moment more and acted.

Straight at the door he bounded. His shoulder, with all his two hundred pounds of bone and muscle behind it, hit the planks. The door flew open with a screech of rending metal and splintering wood and crashed against the wall. Slade was in the room, his eyes slitted against the glare of the light.

At the table sat Rance Horrel and a burly bearded individual. The table was littered with packets of bank notes and stacks of gold pieces. Both men jerked erect to stare unbelievingly.

Slade's voice rang out, 'In the name of the

177

State of Texas! You are—'

His voice was drowned by a yell of rage from Rance Horrel. As Slade jerked his guns, the rancher came to his feet with a rush. His arm lashed out and the lamp flew from the table to smash on the floor. Echoing it was the boom of Horrel's gun. And again a bitter fight to the death was waged in the black dark.

Weaving, ducking, Slade answered the outlaws shot for shot. He heard a gasping cry, the thud of a falling body. A slug ripped his cheek. Another twitched at his sleeve like the questing fingers of a ghostly hand. He fired again and again at the flashes on the far side of the room, until the hammers of his guns clicked on empty cartridges. He crouched against the wall, reloading one gun as fast as his fingers could move. The cocked Colt jutting out in front of him, he peered and listened.

He could hear nothing, sense no movement. Were the outlaws dead or were they playing 'possum, waiting for him to reveal his position? It would be in line with Rance Horrel's cold nerve to do just that. He drew his empty gun from its holster and tossed it to one side. It struck the floor with a clatter.

Fire streamed through the darkness. The cabin rocked to a double report as Slade fired at the flash. From the darkness sounded a choking cough and a thrashing about. Another cough that ended in a whistling sigh, then silence utter and complete.

Tense and ready, Slade waited. Finally he reached far out and tapped the wall with the barrel of his loaded gun. Nothing happened. He raked the barrel along the wall, simulating a stealthily moving form. And again nothing happened. In the distance he heard a patter of fast hoofs. He straightened up, fumbled a match and struck it on the wall, holding it far out from his body. The flicker of flame showed two motionless forms sprawled on the floor. Very definitely, nobody was playing 'possum this time.

The match flickered out and Slade struck another. Glancing about he spotted a bracket lamp attached to the cabin wall. He removed the chimney and touched the flame to the wick. A steady glow filled the cabin as Pedro dashed in with a cocked gun in his hand.

'*Capitan*, I am too late!' he exclaimed.

'No, you got here at just the right time,' Slade replied as he strove to staunch the flow of blood from his bullet-gashed cheek with a handkerchief. 'Just the right time, Pedro. They're both dead and your brothers are avenged.'

'But not by me, *Capitan*, not by me as I had dreamed would be the case.'

'This is much better,' Slade told him. 'The vengeance trail is a bad trail to ride, and taking the law in your own hands is bad business. Think it over and you'll see I'm right.'

'Yes, *Capitan*, doubtless you are,' Pedro conceded slowly. 'And now my brothers can sleep in peace. Muerte Blanca is truly dead.'

'And dead to stay dead, I hope,' Slade said soberly. 'We can do without further resurrections where he is concerned. We'll pack him to town and put him on exhibition, and maybe folks won't be fooled again by some other impostor.'

He ran his eye over the money stacked on the table that miraculously had not been overturned.

'Rather more than was taken from the express car, I'd say,' he decided. 'They must have had a cache somewhere in the cabin. We'll turn it over to the sheriff and he can divide it up as he thinks best. See if there aren't a couple of horses all set to go in the leanto back of the shack. I've a notion the hellions planned to pull out as soon as they had divided the money and stashed it away. Then I vote we take time out to boil a pot of coffee. Should be daylight by then and it'll be easier going to town.'

*   *   *

Marta seethed with excitement when Slade and Pedro arrived and the whole story was unfolded. Gentlemen with hindsight vowed that they always thought there was something off-color about Rance Horrel and had privately believed that Craig Telo got a raw deal. Slade smiled and did not comment.

'Horrel had the makings of a fine and successful man,' Slade remarked to Sheriff Wilson. 'Brains, courage, ability. Everything but honesty. The sort that would rather make one crooked dollar than five in legitimate enterprise. And ended up as that sort usually does. He was splendidly brave and had a mind keen as a razor.'

'But not quite smart enough to go up against El Halcon,' observed the sheriff.

'El Halcon had law and order and the support of honest citizens back of him, and those are things hard to buck,' Slade replied. 'They meant trail's end for Horrel.' He turned to Pedro.

'And I figure it's trail's end for you, too,' he said. 'Trail's end so far as smuggling and such things are concerned. Stay on the right side of the law in every way and you'll be better off. You helped me greatly by locating that cabin and overhearing what was said and I appreciate it.'

'And you avenged my murdered brothers, *Capitain* and I appreciate that,' Pedro replied.

'Show your appreciation by settling down and becoming a good Texan,' Slade said.

'That's right, son,' added the sheriff. 'You and me will have a little talk after a while. I figure I can use you. You're a smart *muchacho* with plenty of everything it takes.'

'Thank you, *Señor* Sheriff,' Pedro answered gratefully, and for the first time since that dreadful day in the canyon, Slade saw him smile.

'Suppose you'll be leaving?' the sheriff asked Slade.

'Yes,' Slade said. 'Captain Jim will have another little chore lined up for me by the time I get back to the post, the chances are. Maybe he's been reading some more poetry and has gotten an inspiration.'

'Poetry!' scoffed the sheriff. 'That old coot wouldn't know poetry if he met it in the road!'

'I'm not so sure,' Slade smiled. 'Captain Jim is full of surprises.'

They watched him ride away, tall and graceful atop his great black horse, to where duty, danger and new adventure waited, an expression of pleasant anticipation on his sternly handsome face. Soon El Halcon would be on the trail again.